Also by Helen Humphreys

Followed by the Lark

Followed
by the Lark

HELEN HUMPHREYS

FARRAR, STRAUS AND GIROUX

NEW YORK

Farrar, Straus and Giroux
120 Broadway, New York 10271

Printed in the United States of America
Published simultaneously in Canada by HarperCollins Publishers
Ltd and in the United States by Farrar, Straus and Giroux
First American edition, 2024

Lark art on chapter title pages from iStock.com / ZU_09.

Library of Congress Cataloging-in-Publication Data
Names: Humphreys, Helen, 1961– author.
Title: Followed by the lark / Helen Humphreys.
Description: First American edition. | New York : Farrar, Straus
    and Giroux, 2024.
Identifiers: LCCN 2023039021 | ISBN 9780374611491 (hardcover)
Subjects: LCSH: Thoreau, Henry David, 1817–1862—Fiction. |
    LCGFT: Biographical fiction. | Novels.
Classification: LCC PR9199.3.H822 F65 2024 | DDC 813/.54—
    dc23/eng/20230824
LC record available at https://lccn.loc.gov/2023039021

Our books may be purchased in bulk for promotional, educational,
or business use. Please contact your local bookseller or the
Macmillan Corporate and Premium Sales Department at
1-800-221-7945, extension 5442, or by email at
MacmillanSpecialMarkets@macmillan.com.

www.fsgbooks.com
Follow us on social media at @fsgbooks

1   3   5   7   9   10   8   6   4   2

For Kirsteen

The only remedy for love is to love more.
—Henry David Thoreau

Followed by the Lark

1822~1838

THE axes were swung at waist height by the loggers, so the stumps they left behind were taller than five-year-old Henry. He stumbled through the forest of stumps towards the shimmer of silver, a colour he had only seen before as gull wing or frog belly.

Pond was what his parents called it, meaning water that you could see across, not the wild, untameable ocean. *Think of it like a large, deep bowl,* said his father.

But Henry could only see the flicker of the water, not its containment. He couldn't compare it to anything. Walden was the first pond he'd ever known, so it might as well have been the wild ocean. All he had was the silver flash, the piney smell of stumps in the afternoon heat, his sister's small hand in his, the push of warm June sun against his back.

This was after they had left the farmhouse for the general store, and then left that for the boarding house, where Henry's father set up a small factory next door and spent his days hunched over a bench, mixing wax and glue with graphite, his hands always black as crows from the lead of the pencils he was making. The crows fluttered up when he was talking, bending the air this way and that above Henry's head.

SCHOOL was a smoky one-room building, where the elderly
Mr. Allen failed to keep order, but was impressive for his ability to know something about everything. When released outside Henry and his friends raced through the fields or went
nutting in the woods, skated over the marshy ice in winter.
They memorized Virgil and the best spot for swimming.

Lime-trees were his, and many a branching pine;
And all the fruits wherewith in early bloom.

Sometimes after school his mother, Cynthia, took her
four children to the pond, where they collected flowers to
slide between the pages of their books, pressing them into
bright coins to spend later, separately, as memories.

The children were close in age and nature. There were just
seven years between eldest and youngest. Sophia had tumbled
after Henry the way that John had tumbled after Helen and
Henry had tumbled after John.

THERE was always music in the house. His father's flute. His
mother's piano. Henry liked to hear the playing flare up in a
different part of the house than the one he was in. How the
music floated up the staircase to his bedroom from the parlour. How it spiralled out a window, twining through the roses
to find him where he wandered in the garden.

When it came time to choose an instrument, Henry decided on the flute over the piano, because he could carry it with him, tuck it into a coat pocket to take out and play as he roamed the hills and woods. Sophia, in her turn, chose the piano and became quite good at it. She often played a song by Mendelssohn:

> *I would that my love could silently flow in a single word,*
> *I'd give it the merry breezes,*
> *They'd waft it away in sport.*

HENRY spent a lot of time exploring the banks of the Concord River that meandered through town. He watched the musquash climbing in and out of their muddy burrows, and envied their glide across the water at sunset.

I'm going to build a boat, he declared one night at supper. *Then I can row out upon the river and truly explore it.*

Henry was sixteen years old. He had repaired fences and window frames, but he had never built anything bigger than a bird box before.

There was silence after his announcement, but it only lasted the moment it took for the rest of Henry's family to catch up to his idea.

Two seats perhaps? said John Sr. He pushed his knife and fork into parallel lines on the tablecloth. *So you could carry a passenger.*

Helen added her cutlery to her father's to show the triangular prow of the boat, and John used his knife and fork to simulate the oars. Sophia grabbed the little mustard pot from

7

the centre of the table and placed it in the middle of the make-shift boat.

There you are, she said. *Happily rowing on the river after supper.*

What will you call your boat? asked Cynthia.

It will be a doorway to adventure, said Henry. *I will call it* The Rover.

At Harvard Henry was put in rooms with Charles Wheeler, the son of a farmer from Lincoln, the town just next to Concord. They had been children together in the one-room schoolhouse, but had not spent much time together as young men. Henry thought Charles's cheerfulness at first to be simplicity, not to be trusted, but this assumption proved false. Charles's mind was sharp and his devotion to learning even deeper than Henry's. He was studying Greek and planned to become a clergyman. They warmed their spirits with talk of poetry and God, and warmed their room by placing a cannonball in the fire until it was red hot and then standing it in a skillet on the floor between them. (Even though the Revolutionary War was long over, its materials were still plentiful, and each student room was given a cannonball for heat upon the start of the Harvard term).

There was no time to explore the woods and fields. Classes were rigorous and there was only a half-day off on Saturday. They both confessed to missing their families.

Shall we walk home and see them then? said Henry, on their fifth weekend at college.

It was over fourteen miles to Concord. Henry got blisters and had to walk barefoot for the last two miles, a cold undertaking in October. But when he opened the front door of the Thoreau home, his family rushed towards him like bees towards blossom. The notes from Sophia's piano piece still hung sweetly in the air, and there was the smell of woodsmoke on John's shirt when he put both arms around his brother and hugged Henry to his chest.

No time for even a bowl of soup, said Charles when they met a half-hour later at the crossroads for the return walk. They needed to be back at Harvard before evening curfew or would be punished for their absence.

Henry's blistered feet, so painful on the walk home to Concord, seemed not to hurt at all on the return journey to the university.

HENRY liked the library at Harvard and the never-ending plentitude of volumes he was able to borrow from it. He enjoyed sitting quietly with Charles in their room in early evening, both of them reading while the light at the window flickered over the pages of their books.

He was not partial to the insistence on academic drills from the instructors, in place of lecture or discussion; nor the raucous activities of the other students. Almost every night, it seemed, he was awakened by drunken laughter and the loud crash of cannonballs being rolled down the wooden staircase outside his room. So, when he became ill during his third year at Harvard and had to return home to rest, Henry was only half sorry to go.

HENRY walked to Fairhaven Cliffs with John. Out of breath from the climb, they threw themselves down in the grass at the top. They were as high as the birds up here, and Henry liked to sometimes think of himself that way, slicing across the face of the cliff or shivering up an air current to hang in the sky above the trees and distant river.

When you're finished your studies, we should finally go on our river trip, said John. He was peering down over the edge. *We could build our own boat. A bigger one than* The Rover. *One suited to an expedition.*

Henry rolled over so he was lying next to his brother. They both looked out below to the band of water looping through the woods.

I have to go back to school before I can finish it, said Henry. He had been suffering from a bout of consumption, the disease that had killed his grandfather, and which afflicted both his father and sister Helen as well.

But you're getting better, said John. *Aren't you? I don't hear you coughing so much in the night. And you climbed up here.*

I couldn't keep up with you.

John was quiet for a moment. *It need not tire you to build it, brother,* he said. *If you do the calculations, I can do the constructing.*

WHEN the school term was over, Charles decided to make a shanty to spend the summer in on the shores of Flint's Pond.

Henry was helping him, and now that his health was better, he planned on staying in the shanty with Charles when it was completed. It was good to be with his friend again, but annoying that Charles was constantly quoting his new guru, Emerson, having heard the philosopher lecture recently on the divinity of Nature.

"Every spirit builds itself a house; and beyond its house a world; and beyond its world, a heaven," proclaimed Charles.

Henry chose a stone to fit on top of the others and lifted it carefully into place. The fit wasn't perfect, so he discarded it and tried another. Building a wall without mortar was a careful business that required patience. Henry found he had infinite patience for the foundation wall and absolutely no patience for his friend's endless quotations from Emerson.

Do we need to hear that—again? he said.

Charles just laughed and came over to inspect Henry's work.

What a good mathematical mind you have, he said, admiringly. And then, because he couldn't resist teasing his friend, he quoted Emerson: *"Oh, how the order of things can satisfy."*

Henry just snorted in response, but the truth was that he knew those words and sentiments well, having listened to Charles talk, and they were actually not far from what he himself believed—that true divinity was found in nature, and that man was closest to the divine when he was himself his most natural.

They were building the shanty on Wheeler family land in the woods overlooking the shores of Flint's Pond. Living in it for the summer was a grand experiment inspired by Emerson's writings on Nature. Henry and Charles wanted to unburden themselves of society in order to become wild children again and receive the holiness of clouds and rocks and water.

The shanty was Charles's idea, but Henry was an equal partner in its execution. It was his measurements they were using for the building, his design for the stone cistern they would fashion to capture rainwater.

He had brought some paper and one of his father's newly made pencils to write down his impressions of living in the shanty, and the content of his and Charles's discussions, but when the crude wooden building was complete and Charles and Henry were lying in their bunks, much as they lay in their beds at Harvard, the talk that flowed between them was too quick and lively to pin down, and Henry quickly lost all desire to try to do so.

The summer passed in a wash of colour and sound, in the feeling of the water on their bodies when bathing and how that coolness lingered for hours afterwards. When Henry moved an arm overhead as he lay in bed, he could still smell the pond on his skin.

In order to remain open to the teachings of Nature, and to be as natural as possible, Charles and Henry did not adhere to a specific routine while at Flint's Pond. They ate when hungry and bathed when they were hot. They might follow the song of a bird deeper into the woods, or read poetry aloud, or simply sprawl on the pine-needled ground, listening to the insects clicking in the air above them. Life became only sensation. They closed their eyes of an afternoon and felt the sun on their eyelids, which became, suddenly, the most powerful, exquisite feeling. For hours they were silent, and then at supper, while cooking a fish in a skillet, they had a passionate discussion about the moths that flitted about the woods and how the tapping they made on the undersides of the leaves when they flew into them sounded exactly like rain—how one sound could belong to two completely different things.

The world that summer was a puzzle and a solace in equal measure, and even though they never remarked on this specifically, Charles and Henry could feel it with every word and glance, every sunrise and sunset they watched together over the rippled waters of Flint's Pond.

1838~1842

ELEN, as the eldest child, often charted the course for her siblings. She became a schoolteacher, and both brothers decided to follow her example. After he had finally graduated from Harvard, Henry returned to Concord to teach at the one-room schoolhouse he used to attend. He was lucky to have landed such good employment, and he was excited to be able to pass on his love of language and nature to his young pupils.

Girls on one side, boys on the other. Henry walked up and down the channel between these two tides, quoting poetry and talking about the architecture of a bird's wing.

Near the end of his second week, he was visited by the superintendent of the school committee, who stood at the back of the room, watching in silence until class was dismissed for the day.

They're not afraid of you, he said, walking over to where Henry was stacking up the spelling cards.

I don't want them to be afraid of me.

You're not punishing them?

They haven't done anything wrong. Henry tapped the stack of cards on his desk for emphasis. *And I don't believe in punish-*

ment, he said. *I believe in teaching them to govern themselves, to mind their own conduct. I'm teaching them about morals.*

The superintendent frowned, unconvinced. *You need to punish them,* he said, *even if they haven't done anything. It is important that you enforce discipline. Children learn better when they fear their teacher.*

That evening at home, Henry discussed his predicament with John.

I cannot teach my methods if I am also meant to be obedient in turn.

And if the students become afraid of you, will you be able to teach them anything at all? said John.

There seemed no way out of it.

The next day Henry chose a girl and a boy at random and made them come to the front of the room and hold out their shaking, chubby hands. He beat those hands with a ruler until they were red and swollen and the children were crying from the pain. After school was out, Henry walked to the superintendent's house and resigned his position as schoolteacher.

HE met Charles's guru, Emerson, on a walk one morning. The philosopher was tall and straight-backed, in his late thirties, with a strong voice and grey eyes the colour of a dove's wing.

I hear that your career as our schoolteacher is over before it began, said Emerson.

Yes. Henry was unsure how much his neighbour knew of his reasons for quitting, so he didn't elaborate.

What are you doing now?

Walking and reading and looking at the world.

Until he said it out loud, Henry hadn't realized that this was exactly what he was doing, that his aimlessness had perhaps more purpose than he had supposed.

Do you keep a journal?

No.

You should. Emerson put a hand on Henry's shoulder. *Even your young mind will forget everything you see. Write it down, Henry. Write it all down.*

HENRY was trying to write a poem about the bluebirds. For two years they had been nesting in the box his brother, John, attached to a poplar by the back door of the Thoreau house. The first year, the female was afraid of Henry and flew off the top of the box every time he opened the door, but gradually she became used to him, and to the movements of his family, and at a certain point he realized that she was learning about him at the same rate that he was learning about her.

When she returned in the spring of the second year, the first time she saw Henry emerge from the house, she sang her song directly to him, and her joyous recognition of him thrilled and moved Henry so much that he wanted to document it.

He had it in mind to describe the winter world in his poem, the world that the bluebird missed when she travelled south. But the words he used to detail his experience seemed instead to be covering it up. Some of his rhymes were strained—*box* and *coax*, *brood* and *wood*, *sky* and *thoughtfully* and it seemed a plodding affair, when he had meant it to be as direct as the bluebird's sweet, short refrain. He couldn't help thinking that the bluebird herself would have made a swifter and better job of describing their relationship as neighbours if she were in charge of the poem.

THE Thoreau household was noisier and busier than ever. Aside from the three adult children—Helen was away teaching—there was Aunt Louisa, who was now living with the family, plus the clutch of regular boarders that Henry's mother took in, and four young boys who were the first boarders for the school Henry and John had started. Things were always on the boil, and if Henry wanted any peace to write poetry or put an entry in his journal, he had to go up to the attic, with the bats and mice, and sit on the bare wooden floor while the spiders swung on their silks above his head.

There were day students as well, including Henry's father's friend Bronson Alcott's daughter Louisa May. In fact, the Concord Academy, run by twenty-one-year-old Henry and twenty-four-year-old John, was so popular, there was a waiting list. The Thoreau school did not hold to the tenets of other schools. There was no rote memorizing and no physical punishment. Students were encouraged to be themselves, with individual traits supported and innovative thinking rewarded.

One of the boarding students, Edmund, had an older sister who was visiting for two weeks. Henry and John had walked out with Ellen separately, and had taken her rowing on the river together. Henry had shown her his poetry, but he had also written a poem to her twelve-year-old brother, Edmund, because he had never seen a more beautiful creature, and in writing the poem, he was determined to address beauty itself through the corporeal presence of the boy.

Edmund, however, was not impressed with the poem, barely glancing at it when Henry thrust it into his hand one night after supper.

And now, here they were, Ellen, Edmund, and Henry, together on this July day, come to see the exhibit of African animals inside a tent in Concord.

The giraffe was the most impressive, his head almost grazing the top of the canvas.

The animal is seventeen feet high, said Henry, reading off the placard in front of the enclosure, *but will be twenty feet when fully grown.*

I prefer the gazelle, said Ellen.

What about you, Edmund? asked Henry. *Do you like the giraffe?*

I like the unicorn.

It's not a unicorn. It's a gemsbok. There is no such thing as a unicorn. A unicorn is a mythical beast.

Well, I like it anyway. Edmund lost interest in the display and wandered off. After a few awkward moments, Ellen followed him.

The poem had ruined things. Henry wished he'd never written it, or certainly never given it to Edmund. But when he thought of the poem, he remembered the feelings that inspired it, and he could not find it in himself to disavow his desire to address beauty through poetry.

The gemsbok had two slender horns emerging out of its forehead, but otherwise looked like a kind of short horse. The gazelle, with its big brown eyes, resembled a deer. There was also a bontebok under the tent, which was a type of antelope. But it was the giraffe that Henry couldn't stop looking at. How strange to have one's feet on the earth and one's head level with the tops of the trees. How did it sleep or drink water? How did it feel, in this tent in the centre of town on this July day, so very, very far from home?

CONCORD was a small town of just over a thousand people. Nothing and no one was very distant from everything and everyone else. The Emerson household was just one street over from the Thoreau household, and since their conversation after Henry quit as the Concord schoolteacher, the men had struck up a friendship and were often in one another's houses.

Henry took his poem about beauty to Emerson. He had titled it "Sympathy." With the recent misunderstanding with Edmund fresh in his mind, he had given up expecting the poem to be understood, but he did want to know if it was any good.

He read the poem in Emerson's parlour at night, with the oil lamp flickering in the corner behind him, the light spilling onto his page and then retreating from it like a tide.

"Lately alas I knew a gentle boy," he said. The words, when he uttered them, shook loose a feeling he didn't wholly understand, and he hoped that Emerson wouldn't notice his quavering voice.

But his new friend didn't say anything during the reading, or after Henry had stopped. There was silence in the parlour except for the thud of a moth on the window trying to get closer to the stuttering oil lamp.

Is it any good? asked Henry, when he couldn't bear the silence any longer.

Yes. It is.

Emerson stood up and went to the window where the moth flailed against the pane. He didn't turn around, but talked instead to the window, with his back to his guest.

I knew a gentle boy once too, he said. *At Harvard. Many years ago now.*

He seemed to be muttering mostly to himself, and Henry couldn't really make out what he was saying.

Is it good enough? he asked.

Emerson came back to his chair and stood behind it.

Yes. It's a very fine poem. I think you should publish it.

You do?

I especially like the part about eternity and walking alone. Can you read that again?

Obligingly, Henry chanted:

Eternity may not the chance repeat,
But I must tread my single way alone,
In sad remembrance that we once did meet,
And know that bliss irrevocably gone.

Glorious! said Emerson, shaking off his introspective thoughts. *I will speak to Margaret Fuller at* The Dial. *She will be very interested to hear about the new young scribe of Concord.*

HELEN arrived home for a visit, and after the evening meal she walked with Henry in the garden.

How much of how you teach is about you? he asked her as they rounded a stand of poplars.

What do you mean?

Well, said Henry, *I sometimes have my students write about a spider in the corner because I am interested in the spider in the corner. Do you think that is a good idea?*

Helen pulled her shawl tighter around her shoulders. It was summer, but she had been feeling a chill lately.

I think that your students will remember your passion about the spider more than they will remember the spider, she said. *And that will end up being the more important lesson for them.*

JOHN and Henry had brought buffalo robes and a cotton tent for sleeping, potatoes and melons and bread for eating. They would drink straight from the river when they were thirsty and boil the water for cocoa before bed. Otherwise, they had just the clothes on their backs, a few books, and a journal to write down the particulars of the trip.

It was the end of August when they pushed their boat away from the bank and began their passage down the Concord, a river that seemed to be a flooded field, as there was so much long grass under the hull of the dory. It was called the "grass-ground river" by the Pennacook tribe, who originally lived where Concord was now.

Henry liked to think of those earlier people travelling the same route as his brother and himself. He tried to pick their camping spots based on whether he thought the Pennacook might have once camped there—a flat rock by the river's edge, an open spot under the pines.

The boat was fifteen feet long and could be rowed or sailed. One of the masts detached so it could be taken off the boat at night and used as a tent support.

Henry and John talked a lot about the boat—how well it steered, how the melons and potatoes made good ballast, how stable it was—and not at all about the fact that they were both spending time with Ellen.

It was a mess in Henry's mind—Ellen, Edmund, the poem, all the feelings that had swirled around the brother and sister—and he preferred not to think about any of it at all. Certainly, talking about it with John, who he knew also had feelings for Ellen, would set nothing to rights. Better to have calming conversations about the strength of the current in the river and which one of the watermelons to eat for lunch.

They named the islands for what they found there. Fox Island. Grape Island. At night they lay in their tent hoping to hear owls or wolves, and instead heard nothing but the barking of distant dogs.

There were willows along the banks, with their fronds trailing in the water and the small leaves turning in the light so that they looked like little silver fishes.

In the mornings there was a thick white mist above the river, which, they had been taught by their mother, signalled a good day ahead.

The river moved them along and the slow drift was pleasant.

They could loll in the boat and feel that the river was taking care of things.

I could do this forever, said John. He had his face upturned to the sun, his fingers trolling in the water. All the time spent building the boat and planning the trip was forgotten for Henry in this moment of revelling in his brother's happiness.

Near the end of their week, it rained, and after the rain they could feel the change in the atmosphere. There was a smell, a metallic tang to the air, and an underlying note of coolness. It was suddenly autumn. Summer had fled, and with it had gone their lazy ease. The slow drift of their journey no longer seemed appealing if the weather was turning colder.

Shall we try and get back in a single day? said John. They were on the faster Merrimack River and could use the current to help shoot them along.

It's fifty miles, said Henry.

But shall we try?

Yes, brother. Why don't we try.

JOHN went in person to propose to Ellen and was rejected. Henry proposed by letter and was also turned down.

Her father doesn't want her to marry a Transcendentalist, said John.

But it is Ellen who has said no, argued Henry. In her letter to him, she had stated that she thought of him only as a friend. She seemed surprised that Henry had asked her to marry him.

But perhaps she had said something entirely different to John? Could Ellen's father, a Unitarian minister, really object so strenuously to John believing that the miracle of life was in the spirit of man, and not confined to the spirit of God?

Henry was not even sure how he felt about Ellen. It was stirred up with how he felt about the beauty of Edmund, and with the poem he wrote in celebration of that beauty. When Ellen rejected John's proposal, Henry's attempt was more connected to John perhaps, than to Ellen. If one Thoreau brother was turned down, then perhaps the second one might not be? Proposing to Ellen felt much like many other things they had done together.

"Sympathy" was published in *The Dial*. This happened shortly after the proposals, and the first good feeling Henry had in weeks was when he held the issue of the magazine open to the page where his poem was printed and felt a flush of pride.

He was a man who well understood a mathematical equation, and the one he took away from the entire experience was that emotional entanglements with other people were disappointing, but writing about them was not.

EMERSON offered Henry a live-in job helping with the children and doing garden work. Since Henry was often round at Emerson's house anyway, he accepted the paid employment. He enjoyed talking with Lidian and playing with young Waldo and Ellen, and he was interested in grafting Emerson's apple trees and having free run of his mentor's library.

He liked wandering the garden and playing his flute, taking Emerson out in the boat on the river of an evening. When

Margaret Fuller came to visit, the apple blossom was in bloom and the scent of it wafted down on them in waves as he rowed her around Walden Pond. She had recently rejected his latest batch of poetry sent to *The Dial*, but he did not mind, because her rejection letter was so wise and generous. *Do not say that Nature is yours*, she wrote. *She cannot be yours until you have been more hers.*

Henry meant to make good use of Emerson's capacious library, but when he settled in at the library desk and took down one dusty volume after another from the shelves, he found them all wanting. Where was the fullness of life meant to be contained within their pages? And how could he sit inside this darkened room when outside all was glory and sunlight and the staggering flight of the bee tumbling from flower head to flower head?

THE Transcendentalists met at Emerson's house once a month in the evening. The group fluctuated, but at its core were Emerson, Bronson Alcott, Henry, Margaret Fuller, and Ellery Channing. Channing was becoming a friend to Henry. He had also been at Harvard, although he had left after only fourteen weeks, and he aspired to be a poet. He had recently moved to Concord and, like Henry, he enjoyed the woods and water around the town. The two men had begun taking long walks together.

Ellery and Henry arrived at Emerson's house at the same time and walked up the drive together.

Don't mention my wife tonight, said Ellery. *Even a polite inquiry into her health will not be welcome.*

Why not?

She's after me to secure employment, and I fear she's talked to Margaret about it. I don't want a lecture.

But we're here to be lectured, are we not? said Henry. Both Margaret Fuller and Emerson were inclined to hold forth on the subject at hand, whatever it might be.

But it need not be a lecture about my wandering ways, said Ellery. He had married Margaret Fuller's younger sister, Ellen, and they had moved to Concord to begin their married life together. Ellery was insisting on his vocation as a poet, but it did not come with any money attached.

One of the benefits of having the monthly meetings at Emerson's house was the generous meal that always greeted the Transcendentalists.

Do I smell ham? said Ellery, when he and Henry stepped into the front hall.

There was ham, and corn, and lettuce, and applesauce, and macaroni, and custard and pears for dessert afterwards.

Margaret and Emerson had already conducted the editorial business for *The Dial*, so the group ate and talked about their continued commitment to the abolition of slavery and to the equal rights of women. The Transcendentalists believed in the fundamental equality of every human being, children included, and were against child labour, or even the punishment of children. Henry shifted uncomfortably in his seat when the discussion veered in this direction. He remembered, very clearly, his brief but harrowing time as the Concord schoolmaster.

The teachings of Nature must begin in childhood, said Margaret, to which everyone murmured agreement.

Henry looked around the dinner table at his friends, happily eating and talking. He marvelled that he was a man with such friends as these. Of all that was miraculous in life, sometimes this seemed to be the biggest miracle of all.

HENRY sailed his boat on the Concord River after supper, playing his flute while the dory drifted along in the light evening air. He didn't play a song, but just loosened a chain of notes to cast upon the water. He liked to think of the music being as natural as the wind or the ripples in the surface of the river. Would a musquash swimming to the opposite bank pause midstream to listen to the tumult of notes spooling towards him? Did the bird sheltering in a tree for the night feel consoled by the flute's trailing song?

Henry recollected lying in the tent with John last summer and listening to the dogs barking night after night. Here was a more pleasing sound to give to the darkening sky, to the beasts settling down to sleep and those setting out to hunt.

JOHN SR. was sitting on the front porch, watching the citizens of Concord pass the house, like an endless slow parade. He liked to share the news of the day with whoever caught his eye, reading aloud from his newspaper, but tonight he was talking with Henry instead, who had come out to the porch after supper in hopes of seeing falling stars later on when full darkness dropped.

They did well to hold on for so long, said John Sr. He was talking about the Seminole War in Florida, which had ended after six years with the Seminole people living there being moved west of the Mississippi to reservation lands, in accordance with President Jackson's Indian Removal Act.

Not just the Seminole people were removed, his father continued, *but also the free slaves from Spain who had set up their communities in Florida.*

How can Jackson remove free men?

Because he refuses to recognize them as freed slaves, but instead calls them "Black Seminoles." John Sr. sighed. *This twisting of language is fooling no one, but it's doing its damage.* He paused. *Are you seeing any stars yet?*

No. Henry was thinking now about the Seminole War, which made it hard to look peacefully at the heavens. When the natural world was overlaid with the human world, Henry often found that the former disappeared into the latter.

1842~1843

O N New Year's Day, 1842, John cut his finger while he was sharpening his shaving razor. It was nothing, just a nick; so slight an injury that he didn't bother to bandage it. But it became sore and stiff after a few days. By the time he showed it to Henry one morning after breakfast, the whole finger was turning black.

It's bad, isn't it? he said.

I think we should call for the doctor.

Henry and his brother exchanged a long, steady look while their shared panic fizzled in the air between them.

By the time the doctor arrived at the house, John was experiencing spasms in his neck muscles and his jaw was clamped shut.

After inspecting his patient, the doctor gathered the family together in the drawing room.

Lockjaw, he pronounced. *Try to make him as comfortable as possible. And write Helen to return back home.*

But there was little comfort for John. His body spasmed uncontrollably, his back sometimes arching so severely that it seemed his spine might snap. His hands clenched into fists and pounded his own chest.

Sophia tried to wipe their brother's fevered brow with a cold cloth, and Henry tried to force some water between his clenched teeth. When Helen arrived, she attempted to massage his feet, which had stiffened into claws.

But none of it did any good. John couldn't talk or be saved from pain. He was often in spasmodic motion and, in the end, the only way to alleviate the bucking was for Henry to hold him tight in his arms and ride it out with him, as though his brother's body was a ship on a stormy ocean and Henry had tied himself to the mast.

Henry pressed himself against the body of his brother, clasped him tight around his heaving chest, while John struggled to breathe. Henry willed some of his healthy spirit to transfer out of his body and enter his brother's, to help make him well, but it did not work. Eleven days after he nicked his finger with a razor, John died, and as he finally lay still in Henry's arms—for which the family felt only relief—Henry sensed some of his own spirit leaving with his brother.

EMERSON came to sit with the grieving family.

I cannot believe it, he said. *Just two weeks ago he was at my house, putting up a bluebird box for the children.*

It had been two and a half years since the river trip, but Henry was flooded with the memory of it. He could taste the sweetness of the melons they ate and see the thick mist over the water. When he lay in his bed at night, he heard the murmur of John's voice next to him as though they were lying together in their tent.

A few days after John died, Henry went to find his sister Sophia in the parlour. She was sitting at the piano, not playing, her hands twisted together on her lap.

I think I have lockjaw, he said. *I am finding it hard to open my mouth, or talk.*

Sophia looked up, and Henry could see that her eyes were red from crying.

Henry, she said. Her voice was soft.

I need the doctor, said Henry. *Please, Sophia. Will you fetch him for me?* He was starting to panic, remembering the twisted shape of John's body in his final days.

Sophia put on her winter cloak and boots and went out into the snowy streets of Concord. She returned with the doctor. Henry heard his steady tread on the stairs as he approached Henry's bedroom.

The doctor felt along his jawline and listened to Henry's heart, examined his fingers and toes for septic wounds.

It is terrible that your brother died, he said finally, *but I don't think that you also have lockjaw.*

Henry could not speak at this point. His teeth were clenched tightly together, and he couldn't pry them apart with facts or logic or his own two trembling hands.

AT the end of January, Emerson's five-year-old son, Waldo, died from scarlet fever. Henry, recovering at the Thoreau home from his bout of phantom lockjaw, trudged across the lawn to Emerson's house and sat with him and Lidian and the children in their parlour. He remembered the bright laughter of Waldo, the games of hide-and-seek they would play together in the garden. Then one small boy became another in his thoughts, and it was John he was searching for behind the rose bushes.

Emerson began working on a poem about his beloved child, and when it was finished months later, he asked if he could read it to Henry. He read it aloud in the library, standing at the window for the light, his back to his young friend.

> *Not mine,—I never called thee mine,*
> *But Nature's heir,—if I repine,*
> *And seeing rashly torn and moved*
> *Not what I made, but what I loved . . .*

THE girl was maybe nine or ten. She banged feebly on the front door of the Thoreau house, and when Henry opened it, he found her standing there.

I was in your school, she said.

The school is closed, said Henry. *Permanently. My brother died.*

Not that school. The one in the village, where you were the teacher once. Where you were my teacher once. The girl stared hard at Henry, but he failed to recognize her.

I was barely there, he said.

The girl put her hand in her coat pocket and pulled something out. She thrust it towards him.

I brought you something.

It was a small bird, a purple finch, lying motionless in her hand.

I thought you might like it. It flew into our window today.

Henry knelt beside her, and she dropped the bird into his palm.

I know your brother is dead, said the girl. *That's why I thought you might like to have the bird.*

The finch felt warm from being in her pocket. Henry touched the blush of its breast, gently stroked the tiny red feathers on its crown.

Thank you, he said. *I like it very much.*

Where do you think it was going? asked the girl. *When it hit our window?*

To its winter palace.

It was October now and the birds were sky-bound. The leaves were scarlet and the winds had a chill to them when Henry walked out at night. The flush of colour on the finch's breast was the same hue that was found on the autumn leaves.

The girl was quiet for a moment.

Do you think the winter palace is as beautiful as the summer palace? she asked.

It's more beautiful, said Henry. *It must be, because the birds leave the loveliness of our summer palace to go there.*

1843~1845

I T was decided that Henry would go to New York and help
tutor Emerson's brother's child and live with the family.
Since Henry couldn't settle to anything in Concord, it made
sense for him to try and find employment elsewhere.

Emerson's brother William lived on Staten Island and
worked as a lawyer in Manhattan. The country house on the
island pleased Henry when he first arrived. He was excited
by the constant presence of the ocean, and liked to go down
and watch the fishermen drying their nets on the beach, and
delight in the scuttle of crabs along the sand in front of his
boots as he walked the shore.

There was not much sympathy between him and his young
charge, but he balanced this out with exploring Manhattan in
his free time—visiting the Mercantile Library and trying to
advance his literary career. He met with several other writers
and found an editor willing to help him place his essays, but
he was homesick and plagued by a nasty cough.

More worrying, Henry started falling asleep at inoppor-
tune moments—over his plate of food in the evening, while he
was trying to teach young Willie, when he was reading a book
or writing an entry in his journal. He couldn't seem to control

the episodes, nor know how long they would last. It began to make almost everything he did impossible.

He told his mother about this new affliction in one of his letters home, and she wrote back to say that she thought this was something from her side of the family. She remembered an uncle who fell asleep in the hallway while putting on his coat.

UNABLE to continue teaching his charge because of the sleeping fits, Henry tried to earn money by selling the new magazine *American Agriculturist* door to door. The city dwellers were perhaps the wrong audience for a magazine that spent pages detailing how to fatten beef cattle or keep sheep from being infested by the gadfly. Even Henry couldn't bring himself to read through the entire first issue. He had few takers.

One night there was a terrific storm, brought on by a hurricane in the mid-Atlantic. There was no boat to Staten Island on a night so rough, so Henry stayed in the city with an acquaintance. They watched the storm together and marvelled at the wild gusts and the ferocity of the rain. At one point toads actually fell from the sky, having been scooped out of the water by the wind and deposited inland on the streets of Manhattan.

When he finally made it back to Staten Island the next day, Henry was scolded by Emerson's brother William for his absence.

You should have sent word to us, said William. *We were worried and searched for you.*

In Concord, if Henry was out overnight, his family would

just think that he was on an adventure so thrilling that it could not be stopped on account of darkness. They would never embarrass him by searching for him as though he were an errant child.

HENRY had accepted the position in William Emerson's household in part because he thought it was what John would have wanted him to do. His brother was never out of his mind, and he felt an added responsibility to John, because he was dead, to live as John himself might have wanted to live. He was certain that John would have embraced the opportunity to explore New York. He would have been bolder than Henry in that landscape and any other, would not perhaps have felt as lonely or as lost as Henry did.

He persevered, but in the month of June, he received a letter from Emerson telling him that Charles Stearns Wheeler had died of gastric fever in Leipzig at the age of twenty-six.

Henry's compass was already orienting towards home, but Charles dying made him more inclined to leave his New York life and head back to Concord. He had tried and failed, since John's death, to live as his brother would have lived. Now he had to add to this the extra responsibility of trying to live as well as Charles, to honour the spirit of his newly dead friend. It felt like an impossible thing to do while he was still on Staten Island.

He returned to Concord for Thanksgiving, and the relief of being once more in the heart of the Thoreau family was so great that he almost felt knocked over by its force.

Could I come home, do you think? he asked Helen. He was lingering over breakfast, fretting, and she was cutting out newspaper clippings and gluing them into what looked like old account ledgers.

Of course, you could, she said, not looking up from her task.

But I made a promise.

They will find another tutor. Henry, you're not irreplaceable. You might not even be a very good tutor.

This made him smile. He looked at what his sister was doing, trying to read the upside-down handwriting in the ledger.

Is this work you're doing for the Society? Helen, Sophia, and Cynthia had become new conscripts of the Concord Female Anti-Slavery Society, in existence since 1837. Helen was its most ardent member, treating every occasion as a reason to flex her morals. She had recently left the Unitarian Church because of its connections to slavery.

I was given these account ledgers from Charleston, South Carolina, said Helen. *They are records of slave commerce, and so I am gluing anti-slavery stories on top of them.* She looked up at Henry. *To make a scrapbook for the Society.*

HENRY had resisted working at his father's pencil factory, but now, with little else in the offing since he had returned home, he set about redesigning the Thoreau pencil—working on the graphite compound to increase the variation in range of soft to hard leads, and changing the shape of the lead itself from square to round, so that it could be sharpened more easily.

Their pencils already had a good reputation, but Henry was determined to make the Thoreau pencil the best in America.

At the same time, he was also trying to write up an account of his trip with John down the Concord and Merrimack Rivers, but unlike the smooth flow of the actual trip, the written version was proceeding haltingly.

In the outside world, the railroad was expanding, and all through the woods and around the edge of Walden Pond were the huts of the Irish labourers, come to work on laying the miles of track and trestle. The new train was to run along the back end of Walden Pond and would be visible, and audible, from practically anywhere on the pond or in the woods.

Henry thought the new encampment looked cozy, and he was not much bothered by a train that wasn't running yet. But when Margaret Fuller came to town for a meeting of the Transcendentalists, she warned him against romanticizing the railroad.

It will change life more than you think, she said.

THE fire had been for their lunch—fish in a skillet, wild garlic, the last of the potatoes from last night's dinner, cooked on a fire in the hollow of an old stump. But the flint couldn't persuade the birch bark into flame. One man struck, the other built the nest of tinder to catch the spark, then they switched, and switched again. Henry and Edward Hoar, five days out on a botany collecting trip and just hours from home. They were delaying their arrival, although neither had voiced this to the other. *Let's try for a fish*, they said. *Let's lunch in the clearing.*

Earlier in the day, Henry had followed Edward down the mountain. When he was offered the lead on the single track, he always declined it, telling his friend that he preferred to dawdle, that there might be a flash of bright flower from the understorey that he would have to investigate. But the truth was that he wanted to walk behind Edward, to watch the body of his friend moving confidently along the trail. Sometimes Edward would whistle a tune, the notes unravelling in the air between his mouth and Henry's ear. All Henry wanted was this moment of being with Edward, but with it came a wild rush of loneliness that bloomed in his chest and made him breathless.

They had stayed up late, talking under the stars, every night of the trip. Edward had said yes to everything Henry had suggested. *Yes, let's bathe in the stream. Yes, I want to explore that meadow.* Not since John had Henry felt such easy accord with someone, and he just wanted to prolong it.

Because the fire didn't spark and catch right away, they heaped the tinder in the stump higher and higher, until suddenly it did catch, and the bundle of bark and shavings popped alight. And then the fire was burning and couldn't be stopped. It tore hungrily through the tinder, raced along the outstretched roots of the stump, barely submerged under the soft loam. The pines cracked and snapped in the sudden heat, their crowns gloriously ablaze.

Edward ran for town, to gather a makeshift fire brigade. Henry ran to warn the nearby households.

But after they had done their duty, they circled back to one another through the burning forest and climbed the ridge above their deserted picnic ground. Below them the fire skipped along the tops of the trees, burrowed into the cords of firewood the nearby households had readied for winter and stacked neatly between the pines.

The men stood close together, shoulders touching. The heat rose and rose around them.

Henry, said Edward, his voice raspy from the smoke and the running. *Henry, look what we've done.*

Henry couldn't quite believe the speed at which everything had happened. He felt numb, but also couldn't stop watching the uprush of the flames.

It was just a fish, he said. *It was only meant to be lunch.*

The fire consumed 150 acres before it was beaten into retreat. It burned through dozens of cords of wood and cost over two thousand dollars in damages to the nearby properties. Henry and Edward were to be prosecuted for starting it, but Edward's father, Samuel Hoar, was one of Concord's most prominent citizens, and he paid the affected landowners for their property damage, so that no charges were laid against Edward or Henry.

AFTER the terrible shame of the fire, Henry decided to leave Concord for a while. He had taken Margaret Fuller's advice to heart, wanting to immerse himself in nature without expectation of what he would find there.

He walked up Mount Monadnock in New Hampshire and then across a portion of Massachusetts. He didn't bring provisions, but ate berries he found along the way, or a loaf of bread he bought from a farmer. When water was scarce, he drank the rain that had collected in the horse tracks. On an especially cold night, he slept under old boards he had scavenged from a ruined building and woke in the morning feeling like he had survived a shipwreck.

After Henry climbed Monadnock, he met up with Ellery and walked in the Catskills and Berkshires with him before heading home. He had been gone for weeks. In Concord his mother and sisters were protesting slavery by demanding that the United States be dissolved. *"No union with slaveholders you followers of the free,"* they sang.

> *Onward, then, ye fearless land!*
> *Heart to heart, and hand to hand;*
> *Yours shall be the patriot's stand,*
> *Or the martyr's grave.*

UNLIKE the shanty he and Charles had constructed on Flint's Pond, Henry's small house would be built close to the water, so he would have no need of a cistern, but could drink straight from Walden Pond.

Emerson encouraged the venture by loaning him the land. Henry cut down trees from the wood and repurposed some old boards from a shack he purchased from one of the Irish railway workers. The foundation and fireplace he made from stone and old bricks, mortared with sand he scooped from the shores of the pond. Most of the work he did himself, although he had friends come and help with the raising of the roof. The farmer Edmund Hosmer, who lived nearby to Walden Pond and was an old friend of Henry's, was particularly helpful during the construction.

The building was ten feet by fifteen feet and contained a bed, desk, table, three chairs, and the fireplace. There were two windows facing one another on either side of the house. It took Henry just over three months to construct it, and he moved in on July 4, 1845. He was twenty-seven years old.

He meant to work on his book about the river journey with John, and to grow a field of beans to sell. He meant to study the creatures of the air and water and woods, to see what or who crossed his path at any given moment. He meant to live as simply and deliberately as possible, and to honour the spirit of his brother and Charles, in doing a thing they would have approved of him doing, and that they might well have done themselves if they were not dead.

1845~1850

THE apple had been in his pocket all day. He could smell its perfume when he bent to examine a beetle, and again when he stretched his arm up to poke at a bird's nest in the branches of a pine. Periodically he took the apple out of his pocket and held the good weight of it in his palm, bringing it to his nose to sniff its sweetness.

The apple was known as a Sopsivine, which was a compressed version of its more formal name, Sops-in-Wine. It was a yellow apple with a blush and a mild taste, but an aroma as strong as the scent of a rose. The name came about because it was sometimes used to flavour wine.

Henry carried the apple in his pocket because he meant to eat it, but he couldn't bring himself to extinguish the fragrance. He also liked to think that while the dead could not taste the food of earth, perhaps they could still smell its perfume? This is what the Greek gods he liked to read about had always lived on, air, and now that John had died and become a god to Henry, now that he dwelt in the heavens, perhaps he could be nourished by the scent of the apple in his brother's earthbound pocket?

THE woodchopper passed by Henry's little house some days. He carried his huge axe slung over his shoulder as lightly as though it was only the weight of a twig. He waved to Henry, and then a few days later, they exchanged greetings. Eventually the woodchopper stopped to chat on his way in and out of the wood. His name was Alek and he was French-Canadian, from the province of Quebec. When he heard that Henry was having problems with a woodchuck eating his beans, he offered a solution.

Just pop it in the pot, he said. *I ate one myself the other day. It was a little greasy, but also very tasty.*

He rubbed his large hands together and grinned at Henry.

If I didn't have to cut trees all day, I would hunt up all the birds and squirrels and woodchucks in this wood. Put them all in the pot!

Henry, who was debating whether he wanted to eat animals at all anymore, and who was cultivating a friendship with the mouse who lived under his floorboards, was shocked by Alek's admission, but also shocked to find that he didn't hold it against the woodchopper. In fact, there was a lot to admire in the boldness of the other man's appetites.

Alek was his first friend while living at Walden Pond, and Henry welcomed the friendship with a kind of ferocity. He found himself lying in wait for Alek in the mornings when the woodchopper might pass by the cabin, so they could say a few words to each other at the start of the day. If he could catch Alek in the evenings, then Henry could sometimes entice him to share a meal, and he would read Homer to Alek or try to teach him the original Greek version. Though the woodchopper had never had any formal education, he had a curious mind and seemed to like the heroic story of *The Iliad*.

Where Henry once thought Charles was simple, and then was proved wrong, he could never truly decide if Alek was simple or had depths that weren't readily available. Sometimes after a lengthy oration on the friendship between Achilles and Patroclus and a reading from Homer to boot, Henry would ask Alek what he thought, and the woodchopper would say only, *It's good*, without elaborating.

But Henry also wondered if it mattered that Alek might be simple. Maybe it was enough to marvel in the woodchopper's strength—he could cut, shape, and pound in fifty fence posts in a single day—and not worry about Alek's scant interpretation of Homer. There was something refreshing in the woodchopper's complete disregard for the niceties of language. With his French accent, he sometimes hacked at words the way he hacked at the timber in the forest, taking several swings before he could land the deciding blow.

HENRY had inherited his brother's flute when John died. He still had his own flute to play, but he liked to take out John's flute periodically. There was a stain like a shadow below the mouth hole on the boxwood from where John's lips had rested when he played. Henry liked to look at that stain. It was proof that his brother had once made music out of air and wood and his breath, that he had existed.

But the longer that John was dead, the harder it became to

conjure up his life and the further away he felt. So, it was not enough to simply look at his brother's flute. Henry began to play it as well, putting his mouth on the spot where John had put his mouth before him, so that, after a while, that stain on the wood became his shadow as well.

John had not made his flute, but he had carved his name into it and the date of 1835, with two little stars, one on either side of the year. While he was living at Walden and playing the flute in the evenings, Henry carved his name into it as well, just below his brother's. He placed the same two little stars around the year, 1845, a full ten years on.

HENRY had always been good at mathematics. While he was at Harvard, using books from the library there, he had taught himself the rudimentary practices of land surveying. If he was to be a writer, he would also need another source of income, and there was a great need presently of surveyors in Concord, as landowners were subdividing their vast tracts into farms and woodlots. It was a job that appealed to Henry because of its exactitude, but also because it would enable him to work outdoors, and to work alone.

He decided to hone his skills by doing a survey of Walden Pond while he was living there. In January the ice was thick enough to walk on, so Henry circumnavigated the small body of water by foot, pausing at various places to look back at the shore. How different the woods looked from the pond! How interesting to see his tiny home as a duck would see it.

He dragged his surveying equipment out onto the ice and

drove in stakes along the shore. He cut over a hundred holes in the crust on the pond and dropped in a line with a stone tied to the end so that he could measure the depth.

It took days to do all the calculations, to draw the intersecting lines in pencil on a piece of paper, to chart the scoop of water that was Walden Pond. Now he could say that he knew how deep it was in the deepest part—102 feet. And where the exact middle was.

When he hadn't known the depth of the middle of the pond, it was limitless. Now it was merely 102 feet. Learning the facts of the pond satisfied a kind of curiosity, but was this curiosity satisfied at the expense of mystery? Perhaps there was more pull towards the pond when it was more mysterious to Henry, when he knew it less?

At the edge of Henry's bean field, right on the lip of the road, was a pile of bricks, all that remained of the small home of Zilpah White, a former Concord slave whose owners left the country and deserted her and her brother, leaving them behind to fend for themselves.

Zilpah had constructed a house in Walden Woods, much the size of Henry's cabin, but she had to live in that tiny space with her animals, as she had no barn or shelter for them. Even though Massachusetts was the first state to abolish slavery in 1790, she was burned out once by townspeople who objected to a Black woman living free. She rebuilt and made a small garden.

Cynthia remembered her singing as she spun cloth in her tiny cabin to sell for her living, although she was soon in competition with the new cotton mill that opened in Concord, and which quickly put anyone with a spinning wheel out of business.

She had a lovely voice, said Cynthia when she came out to Walden one day to bring lunch to Henry and they walked over to inspect his bean field. *You could hear her singing a long ways off, before you set eyes on her.*

Zilpah's brother, Brister, lived with his wife and children in another small house at the top of a hill, and though that house and family were over twenty years gone, the hill was still called Brister's Hill.

Because Walden Woods was situated so close to town, it was, before Henry's tenure there, a refuge for Black men and women who were living free after having been slaves of the Concord elite. Henry liked to think of Zilpah when he was working in his bean field, and of Brister when he went to drink water out of the spring at the bottom of Brister's Hill. Even though these former inhabitants of Walden Woods were no longer there, surely if the wind angled the right way, Henry would be able to hear Zilpah's voice swinging open over the fields. The spirit of a person lived on in the way they lived upon the land, and sometimes those lines into the past could be seen and followed as clearly as if they were marks on a map.

MARGARET Fuller was right. The railroad changed everything. Four times a day the train ran between Concord and Boston, passing across the far end of Walden Pond. It was possible to work in Boston and live in Concord, and so farmland was being carved up into plots for houses. It proved to be a very good time to be a surveyor.

The train, which Henry had romantically imagined as a picturesque addition to life at Walden Pond, was instead a shaking, smoking monster with sparks flying from its wood-powered belly, regularly setting the woods at Walden Pond on fire.

The train always seemed to interrupt birdsong or reverie, to rudely announce the outside world in moments when Henry was napping in a sunbeam, or marvelling in the flight of a butterfly.

HENRY spent two years at Walden Pond. When he left, he went to live with Emerson's family while Emerson was away in Europe on a lecture tour. He read Margaret Fuller's account of her travels on the Great Lakes and decided to follow her example of braiding together many things for the book on his and John's river journey. Why shouldn't a book about the flow of the water be a drifting along itself? Not only should the particular details of the trip go into the book, but also what Henry was thinking and reading at the time.

Helen was living at the Thoreau house now, having fallen ill with consumption. She reassured the family that she was on the mend, but it soon became clear that the opposite was happening and she was dying.

Henry had often wished that he had a photograph of John, so he hired a visiting daguerreotypist to come to the house and make images of both his sisters. Helen submitted to her photograph with good grace, but Sophia fussed over her sitting.

What if I don't like it? she said, grumpily flopping down into a chair. *What if it shows off my worst features?*

I think you might already be showing off one of your worst features, hissed Henry.

It can be done over, said the daguerreotypist. *I can come back at any time of your convenience.*

Don't be too harsh with her, said Helen, after both the photographer and Sophia had left the parlour. She was quiet for a moment. *And Henry, if it transpires that my death coincides with your book being published, please make certain that you celebrate your book, even as you mourn my death. They do not need to be laid one on top of the other.*

Henry's book on his journey down the Concord and Merrimack Rivers with John was released just two weeks before Helen died. She had refused any kind of church service because of the kinship between church and slaveholders, so the family laid her out in the parlour of the Thoreau home. Surprisingly to the family, both of the town's ministers came to pay their respects and perform the funeral in the parlour, a tribute to Helen's goodness. After the funeral, Sophia played some of Helen's favourite songs on the piano, and when she was finished, Henry came over to stand beside his remaining sibling. He felt bereft at Helen's death and couldn't quite believe he would never see her again, nor receive her wise counsel.

Just us now, he said.

The lesser mortals, said Sophia.

It was what Henry himself had been thinking.

Indeed, he said.

Helen and John had been such good people. He was not sure how well he and Sophia, individually, would be able to emulate their elder sister and brother. But perhaps they could join forces and do a better job of honouring them that way.

We must stick together, Sophia, he said. *We must be united.*

Yes, she said, looking up at him. *I have been feeling the very same thing.*

MARGARET Fuller had been in Italy to write and had become swept up in the 1848 revolution of the Italian states that wanted to break free from Austrian rule. She had also, in her travels, acquired a younger husband and had a child, and was bringing her new family back to America. But the ship they were passengers on ran aground off Fire Island in a terrible storm. It took three days for the news to reach Concord. Most people on board survived the shipwreck, but there was no sign of Margaret Fuller or her family.

I should go and look for them, said Emerson, not long back from Europe himself.

He paced up and down the garden. The July flowers were red and yellow sparks behind him.

We should go and look for them, he said, as he made a turn in front of Henry and Lidian, sitting reading under an apple tree.

He strode off down the garden, and when he came back towards them again, he had once more changed his mind.

You should go and look for them, he said to Henry.

IT stormed so hard the rain came down the chimneys and put their fires out. That's what the locals told him when he came looking for the body of his friend. The storm was so powerful it reached right into their houses. There was nothing they could do to help those on the *Elizabeth* as the ship broke open a hundred feet from shore. They could do nothing to help, so they helped themselves to the trunks that rolled up onto the sand, taking jewellery and sewing silk, ball gowns and boots. The bodies they left untouched, each one naked because the rough sea had torn the clothes from the passengers when they were swept overboard.

He saw piles of almonds and juniper berries on the beach. He saw a man with six stolen hats on his head, and bars of soap turned by the waves into cylinders. He found pages from an anatomy text scattered a mile from the wreck, and single gloves packed so tightly with sand, they looked like severed hands. He didn't find his friend, or the metal box with her writing, but her dead child was recovered, so cold and stiff from the sea that the baby waited a whole day to bleed from his wounds.

Afterwards, when Henry wrote up an account of his search for Margaret Fuller for Emerson and the other Transcendentalists, some said he was heartless to record so many details, to ask the thieves for their version of that night. Why was he talking about soap? Where was the feeling for his missing friend?

But a detail was never impersonal—whether remembered or recorded. Paying attention was a kind of devotion, and Henry didn't need to write the words *Love* or *Grief* to prove his tenderness.

For it was Love who strolled along the beach wearing six beribboned hats upon its head. It was Grief that plunged you into a roiling sea, churned you in the waves until your very shape was changed. It was Grief that came down inside your house so hard some nights that all your fires went out.

In October Henry decided to walk Cape Cod with Ellery Channing. The train they travelled on was full of Irish passengers, all of whom disembarked at the cape with Henry and Ellery. The friends followed the line of people to the dunes above the ocean, where the bodies from a recently wrecked emigrant ship had been laid out for identification and burial. October was a time of storms in the Atlantic, a dangerous time to make the passage from Europe to Boston.

One hundred and forty-five famine victims had died within a mile of the shore where they hoped to start a new, prosperous, and less hungry life. Hay wagons carted the bodies up from the beach to the mass grave in a nearby churchyard. Coffins had been fashioned out of bits of wood from the wreck and old barnboard. Some of the boxes were open and some were closed, with red chalk words scrawled on them to describe their contents. *Woman and child. Girl. Young man.*

Henry was surprised to see that the reverend who would be conducting the funeral was none other than Joseph Osgood, the man Ellen had married after she rejected the Thoreau brothers. They spotted one another at the same time. Osgood walked over to where Henry and Ellery were standing.

Not even half of them, he said, gesturing to the bodies laid out on the grass and to the makeshift coffins. *The rest are still trapped under the wreckage. There were a mere handful who survived.*

He moved off to comfort a woman who was kneeling in front of a box, wailing. Henry watched Osgood kneel down to talk with her, the compassionate gesture impressing him.

It seemed strange to witness the aftermath of this ship-wreck, so soon after Henry had walked the beach on Fire Island, looking for Margaret Fuller. But travel by ship was how the world's citizens moved from place to place, and not all of those vessels were well maintained enough to ride out a storm, or captained by experienced sailors.

Days later, Henry and Ellery were walking along the Cape Cod beach when they saw two small boats rowing out from shore. The ocean was calm, and they could see the body of a woman floating upright in the water.

Another poor soul from the Irish wreck, said a man who stopped to watch with them. *The sea is still spitting them out.*

From the shore where he stood, Henry could see the hair of the woman lifting in the swell. He knew it was not his friend, but he couldn't help feeling it was Margaret Fuller, walking across the ocean floor from her shipwreck to this one, through the wild, untameable sea.

1850~1851

SPRING brought floods to Concord. The rivers swelled and the meadows swamped. Henry enjoyed hearing the story of an adventurous brindle cow who, feeling unhappy with the water creeping through her field, left it, crossing a bridge to enter a neighbouring pasture on higher ground. When that farmer tried to chase her off, she decided to take to the river, swimming over it and then wading through flooded ditches until she somehow, miraculously, made it back to the field where she had started.

WITH Helen's death, and to honour her legacy, the Thoreau family increased their activity in the anti-slavery movement and became a stop on the Underground Railroad, sheltering slaves for a night or two before putting them onto trains heading north into Canada. But with the Fugitive Slave Law recently passed by Congress in September of 1850, escaped slaves could now be caught in a free state and returned to their southern owners. There were more slave hunters coming through town, looking to collect the rewards that the slave owners had posted for their runaway slaves. Rewards typically ran as high as a few hundred dollars, which for some men was equivalent to an entire year's worth of wages. There were also policemen from Boston who operated as slave hunters while on the job as policemen. The journey of a slave from captivity to freedom had become more perilous than ever, but the Thoreaus were determined to do as much as they could to ensure a safe passage.

HENRY was in demand as a surveyor and was now making enough money to support himself, and to travel whenever possible.

He was curious about Canada, both as the place where the free slaves travelled to and as Alek's birthplace. He and Ellery decided to go and see what it was like, taking a train north, then a boat across Lake Champlain into Quebec. They were constantly on the move, so impressions didn't have time to settle, but came on one after the other so quickly that things were noticed rather than felt.

Henry liked to say that the only thing he got from going to Canada was a cold.

They saw the Great River and Chaudière Falls, lodged with farmers, tried to speak a mangled French, and when that wasn't understood, they drew what they wanted to express on tablecloths and in the pages of their notebooks.

Henry hoped to understand Alek better by going to his homeland. If he bathed, even briefly, in the French-Canadian culture, then it would make them equals on some unseen level, and their friendship would be changed by this new equality.

Alek had once accused Henry of being cold and standoffish, of not saying how he really felt. He could never explain to the woodchopper that for Henry, it wasn't about simply express-ing his feelings. What he wanted was to be equal in the same moment with another, then all was felt and mixed together and understood completely, without having to say a word.

HE found the buttercup on Bear Garden Hill. A pip of bright-ness in dun-coloured November. Henry knelt down beside it to better appreciate the oddity and miracle of a spring flower still holding on to its patch of hillside in late autumn.

Sometimes there was a return to spring in October, with a string of warm days and the second bloom on a rose, with the sun still celebrated within the head of a sunflower or hawk-weed. But a spring flower in the last week of November, a breath away from winter, was another thing entirely.

Henry collected plants for the herbarium he was making with his sister, and he was tempted to pluck the November buttercup and bring it to show her, to press it carefully and preserve it for posterity. But the bravery the little flower had displayed by growing so far out of season was perhaps better appreciated by leaving it be. So, Henry unfolded himself to standing height, tipped his hat to the splendour of the butter-cup, and moved on.

THE dentist made a vulcanite mould of the inside of Henry's mouth, top and bottom. He would stud those moulds with porcelain teeth and harden them in plaster, ready to slide back into Henry's mouth after all of his natural teeth had been pulled. At thirty-four Henry was younger than other people he knew who had to have false teeth put in, but tooth decay was commonplace everywhere. Most people would have some, if not all, of their teeth replaced before they had become old.

The ether was not what he had expected. The backwards flip his mind made was not the gentle ease of sleep, but something darker and deeper, an obliteration of conscious-ness rather than a slip away from it. When he awoke, it felt as though he had been hibernating through winter.

The teeth were much more comfortable than he had thought they'd be, and were, in fact, much more comfortable than the rotten teeth they had replaced. Henry wished he'd done it sooner.

The differences were subtle, but he noticed them immedi-ately. The new teeth heated up and cooled down at a slower rate than his natural teeth did, so if he wanted, he could now drink hotter or colder liquids. Also, when he tapped the new teeth with his finger, he couldn't feel any sensation.

I am becoming less human, he said to Sophia.

That may be, she replied, *but your less human parts are nicer-looking than the human parts they have replaced.*

THE crabapple on Emerson's property had come into flower, great pink drifts of blossom and a wheel of scent that rolled towards Henry as he walked towards the tree. He liked to stand beneath it with his eyes closed, listening to the whir of the bees as they fumbled the blossoms above his head.

Crabapples were the only native apple tree to North America. All of the thousands of other apples were brought from Europe and then bred into their infinite variation on American soil.

So, the crabapple tree spoke directly to the land whence it came—this one in Emerson's garden, and another that Henry had heard about from farther south, a small green crabapple called Michaux, where the apples carried the same intense perfume as the blossoms. O, to drink the cider made from these small apples. It would make a human into a bee for one delicious, intoxicating moment.

HENRY hired a horse and wagon to haul his surveying equipment to a nearby woodlot. The surveying work was satisfying on multiple levels. He enjoyed the mathematical problem of working out the lines and angles and distances of a property. And he liked to see into different pockets of the countryside.

The farmer who was hiring the wagon out to him was hitching it up to his horse, while a black and white dog wove in and out of the horse's legs.

Don't mind him, said the farmer, *but he'll likely go with you on account of his friendship with the horse.*

True enough, the dog trotted beside the horse out to the woodlot, lying down beside it in the shade while Henry made his measurements. When most of the work was done, Henry

73

sat on a stump and shared his lunch with the animals, tossing a crust of bread to the dog and pressing a bit of apple into the horse's mouth.

You're a fortunate beast, he said.

It was as nice to be in the company of such fellowship as it would be to experience it for himself. Henry was surprised at this, at how content he felt walking back at the end of the working day in the company of the horse and the dog, in the company of the best of friends.

HENRY was swimming in the rain. He liked the sensation of the water all around him, above and below, as though, for an instant, he was completely one with the water. This little stretch of river had telegraph wires strung overhead, and when Henry swam under them, the vibrations along the lines sounded like a harp being played. He floated on his back beneath them, closing his eyes, the rain falling on his face and the human music of the telegraph wires buzzing above. Everything was equally exquisite in that moment—the swimming, the rain, the river, the song of the civilized world—which was how Henry knew that he would remember it forever.

THE man dined with the family, and after lunch they moved to the parlour, where Sophia played the piano while they waited for the hour when Henry would take the escaped slave, also called Henry, to the train station.

But when Henry went early to the station to make sure that the way was clear, he saw a man loitering on the platform who seemed suspiciously like a Boston policeman.

We will try again in the morning, said Henry, when he arrived back at the house. *You will be safe enough here tonight.*

Later, he showed Henry up to the attic.

You have my bed, he said. *I will sleep on the sofa downstairs.*

Henry Williams shook his head slowly.

No, he said. *I don't want to be putting you out of your bed.*

Please, Henry said. He hesitated at the top of the attic stairs. *It's strange that we have the same name,* he said.

My name is the name of my father, said Henry Williams. *He always said I could buy my freedom from him, but he kept raising the price when the time came.*

Henry lay on the sofa in the parlour and listened to the faint footfalls of Henry Williams above his head. He thought about how difficult it must be for Henry Williams to rest, to trust that where he slept was really safe. Henry lay awake until the footfalls subsided, determined to keep Henry Williams company from two floors below.

The next morning there was no one lingering suspiciously around the train station when the two men stood on the platform waiting for the train that would take Henry Williams through Burlington to Canada. Officially, a Black citizen was permitted to travel by rail in Massachusetts. Unofficially, because of reward hunters, the way onto the train was often rife with peril.

How did you get so far north without a map? asked Henry. He knew that Henry Williams had escaped from a plantation in Virginia.

We follow the stars, especially the North Star. And the tele-graph lines.

Henry thought of his recent swim.

The lines make a sound, he said. *Like a harp singing.*

All those wires full of conversation, said Henry Williams. *Perhaps some of it even about me.* He grinned at Henry.

When the train rumbled into the station, they shook hands and then Henry Williams climbed up the steps into the carriage.

Good luck, said Henry, which seemed a feeble thing to say, but he meant it wholeheartedly.

1851~1853

E MERSON, who initially advised Henry to keep a diary, now complained that he was writing in it too much.

You are spending all your energy there, he said. *There will be nothing left over for important work.*

Where once Henry would have followed Emerson's command to burn his poetry that wasn't good enough, now he began to doubt his friend's counsel. Emerson had a lot of ideas about how Henry should behave that, increasingly, didn't have much in common with how Henry wanted to behave.

Also, Emerson said, *you walk alone too much. How will you ever cultivate the right company when you are always solitary?*

I only need the company of a leaf on the breeze, said Henry, which infuriated Emerson further.

Henry couldn't tell his old friend the truth, that he didn't like walking with most people, including Emerson, because they couldn't seem to remain in the moment they were in and their chatter lifted him out of the present, and the whole experience then became completely unsatisfactory.

Ellery, with whom he walked in Cape Cod and Massachusetts, was Henry's preferred companion these days, because he seemed to be the only human who could be present. This was helped also by the Newfoundland puppy that Ellery had recently acquired, who could not help but be in the moment as he barked at stumps with limbs still attached, or bit at the ripples in the river. The townspeople had taken to referring to the puppy as The Professor, insinuating that of the two beings—Ellery and the Newfoundland—it was the dog who was the more intelligent.

Although Ellery had had poems published in almost every issue of *The Dial*, he still had not found steady employment, and in addition to his wife, he now had three children to support.

I am envious of your freedom, he said to Henry.

Henry, who was working more than ever these days, didn't feel free at all.

HENRY surveyed a woodlot and talked to the farmer who owned it about the destruction of the forests.

It used to be that I would know where I was in the woods because of the old trees, said the farmer. *But now that they've all been cut down, the young growth all looks the same and I get lost.*

Henry decided to do his own survey of the Conantum Swamp, measuring any tree that had a circumference of three inches or more. He wrote down his discoveries, noting the number of each type of tree that fell within these specifications:

Bass 6
Black ash 8

Elm 16
Red oak 2
White ash 2
Walnut 3
Apple 5
Maple 9
Hornbeam 2
Swamp oak 1.
Also Dogwood and perhaps Winterberry.

If all the old trees had been logged, then he would set about to learn what he could about the young ones. It became an extension of his surveying habits, and he started to measure whenever he desired to know more about something. It felt reassuring to know the number of trees, or the width of a stump.

HE was surveying in the Ministerial Swamp when he discovered the fern. First he saw seven black ducks and thought that is what he would write down in his journal that evening— seven black ducks flying up out of the bog, taking to the air together like twists of black ink against the clear sky. It was only after he had pounded in the last stake and was standing to wipe his brow, was stationary for a few minutes, that he noticed the fern. It twined around a goldenrod so tightly that they seemed at first glance to be the same plant. But when Henry inspected closer, he saw that the vine had compound fern-like leaves, and when he got home and looked it up in his plant encyclopedia, he found that it was a rare climbing fern, the only climbing fern that was native to North America.

HENRY sat on an oak stump by his old house site at Walden Pond. The little house was gone. Since the land had been Emerson's, he had sold it to his gardener, who later sold it to a farmer who moved the cabin to his land to store grain in. All that was left of Henry's small home was the depression near his feet, where the cellar had been filled in with earth and rocks.

It had only been four years and yet everything had changed. The house was gone as well as any reference to it. The stump he was sitting on was once a big oak. Henry remembered it from his time living at Walden Pond. It was sobering to sit here and to think that he would disappear just as quickly as the oak when his time came.

When he listened for the sound of a bird in the forest, all he heard was the steady beat of the woodchopper's axe.

In the distance he could see the feathery tops of the white pines, shifting with the breeze like green sails in the ocean of sky. The pines had not changed, were still where they always were. So, Henry put his focus there, on the distant majestic trees, and not on the crater at his feet or the splintered remains of his former friend the oak.

HENRY hired an older Irish man to help him with his surveying jobs, but quickly despaired of his new assistant on the first day. The man knew no more than a boy and yet had none of the grace of youth. He was clumsy and dropped a plumb line in the swamp, forgot a length of chain on the stump where he ate his heel of bread for lunch. When Henry told him what to do, the man only remembered half of it, yet told Henry a lengthy story in the middle of the working day about how there were wild horses on an island in the Atlantic, and sometimes, when an emigrant boat from Ireland was shipwrecked there, the Irish passengers ate the horses.

Before he came to work with Henry, the Irish man, Thomas, had worked stacking wood and then hauling rocks to clear a field. All of the work better suited to a man of twenty than one of sixty.

Why did you not learn a trade when you arrived here? asked Henry. At least if Thomas knew how to do one thing, he could make a better life for himself and his family, instead of constantly switching between jobs that were too much for him and that he seemed to know nothing about.

I was too old, said Thomas. *By the time I got to America, I was too old for a trade. No one wants to take on an old apprentice.*

AFTER Christmas dinner was over, Henry climbed up Fairhaven Hill to watch the sunset. Even though it had been years now since John died, the holidays always floated his death to the surface once more and created a kind of restlessness in Henry that was only cured by hard walking or climbing.

At the top of Fairhaven Hill, above the cliffs, the sun was filtered through clouds and angled its rosy light into the windows of all the houses below, so that it seemed there was a candle burning in each window, a light to welcome back the dead.

THERE was an old man whom Henry would sometimes see when he was out surveying. This man lived in a pile of sticks that he had fashioned into a burrow. He had lost both feet from frostbite one winter and hobbled around on the stumps that were left. He would work for drink and lived on berries and small game. There seemed to be no one to whom he was tied, by blood or obligation or friendship. Those who knew of him pitied him, but Henry sometimes wondered if this man had a kind of wisdom that was only available because of his extreme solitude. What did he see that others couldn't? And if Henry had remained forever at Walden, would his life have eventually resembled that of this man?

The old man died one winter, but was found in the spring, his body so badly decomposed that it had to be pitchforked into a coffin.

THE spring weather was warm enough for walking about at night, and so Henry took to the woods after sundown, to see how the night world differed from the day world. At first it was the sounds he noticed—the lack of birdsong, the rising quiver of frogsong, the hoot of an owl, the screech of a fox. At night there was not the green of daylight. Green became brown or black. Water took on the colour of the darkened sky. What seemed so solid in daytime was shifting in darkness. So, Henry felt himself shift. His night thoughts were not the same as his day ones. They were darker, less distinct. One thing ran into the other, and he didn't worry about trying to separate them.

THE light of June was silver and the light in August was gold. Each lent its hue to the plants that presented themselves in those months, and while it was difficult to prefer one cast over another, Henry liked how the silvery June light aligned to the froth of blossom, to the white flowers of stitchwort, the underside of willow leaves, the mist above the river. When he heard the distant strains of a clarinet at dusk, that too belonged to the silvery realm, as did all of music—surely the best thing that human beings had ever fashioned? The notes drifted towards him and were a kind of blossoming, no different from the unfolding of a flower.

ON a hot July day, Henry walked along the bottom of a riverbed. The water itself was so warm that he fancied he could boil eggs in it. First he swam, and then he walked a good length in one direction, turned, and walked back in the other direction.

The riverbed was full of hills and valleys. Sometimes he was in water up to his knees, and then the floor dropped and he was immersed up to his neck. He could look through the murk as he walked, see the dark lines that were bits of sodden wood, the dark circles that were rocks. The fish nests were a kind of underwater hive constructed from sand and pebbles. The fish themselves sometimes darted towards his bare legs, not so much nipping him as running straight into him with their snouts.

Above him the birds floated in the sky, and Henry marvelled at the miracle of inhabiting two worlds simultaneously, much as a mind has a conscious and subconscious, or a day contains both light and dark.

MORE and more Henry was walking alone in nature, communing with the flowers and the birds, noticing the subtle changes in the meadow or understorey. The more he was without human company, the more he believed he was communicating more purely and absolutely with nature, and he began to doubt that this amount of connection would be possible if he were walking the riverbed or the woods with a fellow human. He hoarded his experiences and impressions during the day and then at night wrote them up in his journal. The page became his intimate as much as the lily and the bream and the bobolink. It waited patiently for his attentions all day and then absorbed everything he had to give, leaving him spent and replete by the time he laid his pen down and closed the book.

HE heard it through the open window at noon as he was moving from parlour to bed chamber—still chasing morning thoughts—to fetch the book he had nodded off over last night.

The flight of notes was bright as any birdsong and it stopped him as he crossed the room. Who played the piano so beautifully, and what house contained such music? Which open window on the street released the rush of song towards his open window? He could not answer these questions, nor know what composer had first laid down the lilting notes as flickers of ink on a page. The music floated free of all that would have tied it to earth. It floated free and found Henry where he was—at noon in the family home on his daily rounds. He stood still and listened, every part of him fizzing to attention, and when the piano stopped as suddenly as it had begun, he felt bereft. To have been met, even for an instant. To have been found. To have been filled to the brim.

IT was the end of summer and the river was too full of weeds now for walking. The flowers had grown tall and straggly in the fields. The golden net of light was laid down over everything.

In the dog days Henry thought briefly about dogs themselves. He knew many solitary men who kept them as company, and he wondered about doing this himself. A man he visited recently said he kept a dog to stir up the air in the room, to avoid the atmosphere becoming too still and stagnant. Henry could see the sense in this. Also, to have a companion who existed entirely within the present moment and didn't talk through it was tempting.

But then Henry remembered the dogs barking through the nights when he and John were on their river trip. And he thought of Ellery's dog running after every chipmunk and rabbit he spied. Dogs got in the way of nature, or were interested in it for their own purposes. While being good company, they might put up a barrier to Henry's experience of the wild world.

SOMETIMES when Henry surveyed a woodlot or property, the owner wanted to come along with him. This was not ideal, as part of the appeal of surveying was to be out in nature alone. Having someone tag along with him meant that Henry wouldn't be able to notice much of anything, and he resented this.

But the landowner who insisted on accompanying him on this winter morning was so full of opinion and drink that he was almost as entertaining as a muskrat or fox kit, or the summer night frogs.

Cider was the preferred drink of this man, and he was convinced that the cider was curing him of some unknown ailment. As they walked through the forest, he wondered aloud what else he could use to make alcohol and tasted some juniper berries to see if they might be suitable.

Not bad, he said. *But gooseberries might work better. Perhaps huckleberries too.*

I'm not sure you can make alcohol out of everything, said Henry.

Oh, I think you can. And I mean to try.

They continued through the woods. Henry scanned the trees for birds, and Joshua scanned for anything that could be turned into drink. There was snow on the ground, but it wasn't deep.

Only robin snow, said Joshua.

What's robin snow?

Keeps the robins around for the winter. Not enough to drive them off. If there's a lot of snow at the start of the year, they will just leave.

That night, when he was home and up in his attic, writing in his journal, Henry thought about this comment. It pleased him that someone as fond of drink as Joshua was still connected enough to the nature around him to notice the correlation between snowfall and the behaviour of the robins.

HENRY often took breakfast with his family. They were similar in habit and attitude to one another, sometimes talking about the snowfall, or the antics of the cat, and other times silently reading the newspaper or a book. The Thoreau house was not a house where discord was much in attendance. They were a family, Henry thought one morning when all four of them were sitting quietly around the table, lost in their own thoughts, but they were also a club who believed in the same tenets. It was a fortunate group of people to have been born into, and if Henry hadn't been born into them, he would have sought them out for friendship.

ONE thing was often another. The light of the train through the window looked exactly like the star rising in the north. Henry's steps in the snow sounded like the creaking of a wagon. A bell five miles off had the same hollow quality as the call of the hunting owl.

HENRY had a great deal of ambivalence around the eating of his fellow creatures. He tried mostly not to do it, dining on plain rice or bread when he was camping out on walking trips, but sometimes when eating with his family, the consumption of animal flesh was expected and therefore unavoidable.

When a cousin asked him to come on a hunting trip in Maine, Henry decided to go. He was interested in the idea of only killing to eat and in the fact that his cousin George would be hiring an Indian guide for the trip.

Joe was a member of the Penobscot tribe and was going moose hunting anyway on his own, so was easily persuaded to come with Henry and George for some extra money. After a complicated journey of wagon, stagecoach, boxcar, and steamer, they set out in Joe's birchbark canoe in intermittent rain. Henry found sitting in the canoe uncomfortable, but spent the time trying to get Joe to tell him the Penobscot names for the various bits of nature they were passing. At one point Joe whistled a tune.

Is that a tribal song? asked Henry.

It's "Oh! Susanna," said Joe.

They found no moose that day. After they had set up camp and eaten supper, Henry sat down beside Joe, who was staring into the fire. He started his chain of questions, but Joe held up his hand to stop them.

I don't like to talk after eating, he said.

The next day they found a female moose and her calf in the shallows. George shot the mother, who struggled off into the forest. The calf escaped. They tracked the moose and found her half an hour later, dead at the edge of the shoreline. Joe skinned her with a penknife while her body quivered with the last flicker of her life. The moose was still lactating for her baby, and her death seemed pointless to Henry, as they couldn't take any of the meat with them in the canoe for fear of overloading it, so they only took her hide and left her bloody corpse behind, bobbing in the water.

This was not what Henry had imagined when he had agreed to go on the hunting trip. He had thought of the animal dead, not of the animal dying. The suffering of the mother and baby upset him deeply, and the only way he could think of to calm himself was to fall back on what was familiar and therefore comforting to him. The one thing that helped make the out-of-control situation feel more in control.

Before the moose was skinned, Henry surveyed her. She was eight feet and two inches long from nose to tail. Her ears were ten inches long, and her head was two feet and two and a quarter inches from the base of her ears to the end of her soft nose. The moose was seven feet and five inches from hoof to shoulder, sloping to six feet and eleven inches at the middle of her back. Her foreleg was four feet and nine and a half inches, and the measurement from her nose to the breastbone was four feet and three and a half inches.

That night Henry sat glumly in front of the fire, watching the sparks. Joe, perhaps feeling sorry for him, tried to start a conversation, but it went as badly as all their exchanges.

What do you do on Sundays? asked Joe.

I go for a long walk, said Henry. *I go into the woods and walk among the trees.*

You don't go to church?

No. Nature is my church.

Well, you'll go to hell then, said Joe, getting up and moving off to sit by himself and smoke.

The next day was Sunday and there was no hunting. They paddled to a logging camp where George and Henry planned on staying while Joe went to meet up with some of his people, but Henry hated the crudeness of the men in the logging camp, and after one night there, he took Joe up on his invitation to accompany him to the Penobscot camp instead.

George and Henry sat around the fire with the men gathered there. They didn't seem to mind Henry's questions, and he took notes while he talked with them.

What does Penobscot *mean?* he asked.

Rocky river, replied a hunter named Tahmunt.

And Musketaquid? Henry was interested in knowing the meaning of some of the familiar names of places and geographical features in Concord.

Dead water, said Tahmunt.

When he grew tired and went to bed, Henry lay awake listening to the fluidity and quickness of the Penobscot's conversation with one another, when they no longer had to draw out slow words for Henry to understand.

HENRY wrote a letter for an Irish man who was sending instructions to his wife and children about the crossing.

Tell her to hold on tight to the babies, because it is easy for them to be pitched overboard, the train worker said, and Henry dutifully wrote this down.

Two nights later Henry followed a skunk for about a quarter of a mile, walking behind the animal slowly as it was ambling side to side up the road. He was trying to learn about its skunkness, but was thinking mostly about the Irish man's letter to his wife. Where did she think she was going? What was in her mind when she thought about this place? What is the story we tell ourselves before the real story begins?

The skunk, nosing into a hole in a wall, patting the ground under a tree, was clearly completely at home in this little kingdom it patrolled. How long did it take to be at home somewhere, for the idea of home to stick like a burr on a sleeve?

1853~1855

THE bluebirds still came every year to the box that John had put by the back door of the Thoreau house. Henry always waited for someone in town to say they had seen the first bluebird of the year, and then he knew to pay special attention to the box out back.

He and Sophia had developed a shorthand for their nature encounters. Sophia was just as interested in the birds and flowers as her brother. She sketched and painted them and collected specimens for their shared herbarium. She had even made a chessboard for a friend with tiny ferns pressed into each of the squares on the board.

Bluebird, he said when they passed on the stairs.

Catkin, she whispered to him at dinner.

SINCE he left his little house at Walden Pond, years ago now, Henry had been writing about it. Some of the book was completed while he was living there, but most of it was written afterwards, and in writing about that time, he also, invariably, added in observations from the moment he was presently in, so that the book was becoming as much about his experiences in everyday nature as it was about the specific time at Walden.

The book was published on August 9, 1854. Henry was not sure how he felt about it when it came out. The moments of writing it had been satisfying, but reading it all together, when he was so far past some of those moments, was less so. He noted its publication in his journal alongside the fact that the elderberries had ripened and the climbing bittersweet was yellowing. When he looked down at the entries after having written them, they took up equal space on the page. The publication of *Walden* was not, perhaps, any more important than the berries or the bittersweet as an occurrence in Henry's universe.

HENRY took two people to see his climbing fern, a stranger and a friend, two days apart. First he took his friend Edward Hoar.

Let's unclimb the fern, said Edward, when they got there. *To see how it works.*

They stood on either side of the goldenrod plant where the fern had attached itself, each of them pulling a little away and then passing the vine to the other, slowly and carefully unwinding the fern from its host. They didn't speak as they did this. They had known one another long enough that they were equally comfortable in silence as in speech. It was like stitchery, thought Henry, as the vine was passed to him and he unwound and passed it back. Unstitchery.

They laid the fern out on the dirt between them.

It's longer than it seems when it's climbing, said Edward.

When laid out, the fern looked more like simple ground ivy. The full splendour of the vine came from its reach. Henry wondered if every plant moved into space in the way that best suited it.

They had wound it back up onto the goldenrod by the time Henry brought the visiting botanist, John Russell, to see the climbing fern. The previous evening, at a friend's house, Henry had looked through Russell's microscope at a stalk of rhubarb and had seen all the tiny red fibres and cell craters that made up the stem. Now he wanted to give Russell something in return.

But the visiting botanist wasn't too keen on the walk through the swamp to get to the fern, and when they did get there, he spent twice as long telling Henry about a nearby fungus as he did admiring the fern. It was hard not to feel disappointed, although now Henry at least knew the Latin name of *Boletus*.

It was the coldest winter they could remember. Days and days of a wind so sharp that they couldn't go three steps from the front door before turning back. The milk froze in the pail. The spittle froze on their lips when they tried to talk. When Alek tried to cut down a chestnut tree in front of their house, his axe broke. The family huddled by the fire through most of the day. At night their beds were weighted down with so many bedclothes that they were pinned there like moths for the whole miserable night.

But there was one member of the household who did not

change her routine, who would not bend to winter. The cat left the house every morning, struggling across the snowy yard to the barn, where she hunted mice until nightfall, returning to the warmth of the fire at supper. Was it habit or hunger that made her face the brutal chill? No one knew, but her bravery was admired. What a heroic figure she was, cutting through the snow, her whiskers crusted with ice, her joints stiff with cold.

One evening while they were hunched over their supper plates, the cat strolled by. She had just returned from outside, and the cold drifted up from her fur like smoke. She smelled of the snow, but also of the hay stored in the loft of the barn.

While other households might enjoy a cigarette or brandy after dinner, the Thoreaus pushed their plates aside at the end of the evening meal for a different ritual. One of them would scoop up the cat, and they would pass her from person to person around the table, each of them burying their face in her fur, inhaling the sweet smell of hay, the dried grasses and wildflowers twined together and still carrying the potent scent of summer's ease.

HE had not seen the white owl that others had seen twice now. Nor the white rabbit chased by Brown and his dog that afternoon. The rabbit looped out to try and tire the dog, but then made its way right back to where it had first been sighted.

They do that, said Brown. *Come back to where they started.*

For a while the rabbit was so far distant that the dog's barking was impossible to hear.

Henry thought, Why wouldn't the creature come back to what was probably its home? Familiar ground might feel safer. The rabbit would know what to expect of it and this knowledge would help him to escape the dog. But Henry didn't say this, nor what else he was thinking, which was that the white rabbit was made from winter and that was why Brown could never find its marks in the snow or spy its form huddled on the ground. It was only when the dog had the scent that the rabbit could be hunted. Before that it was as much a part of winter as any drift or snow-blossomed twig.

In spring Henry often felt lonelier than at other times of the year. Aunt Louisa's friend Miss Minott said it was because in spring the sap was moving in all the trees, and the human body was in sympathy with this and it was unsettling. She was told this by her doctor, who was, ironically, called Dr. Spring.

The spring feelings are disturbing, she said.

Indeed, Henry felt his pulse quickening with the lengthening days and the return of the birds, with the leafing out of the trees and the whir of the poplars, the trembling song of the frogs in the marsh.

Sophia found Henry in the garden.

Moth, she said, turning back for the house. Henry followed her inside and up his attic staircase. At first he thought she meant there were moths eating his clothes in his room, but she pointed to the window. A few weeks ago Henry had pinned a cocoon he'd found to the window frame, and the moth had split open the fragile shell of that carapace and was sitting on the glass, slowly opening and closing its new wings, testing them.

Do you think they know when they make the cocoon that one day they will emerge from it as a different creature? asked Henry.

Sophia considered the moth, tilting her head from one side to the other. *I think they know something is going to happen*, she said. *That the long sleep is the middle of the journey, not the end of days.*

EDWARD's father had heard there was a white robin with her nest in an apple tree. In spring a bird that was white should have been easy to spot, but when Henry went looking for her, he couldn't find her. Every apple tree housing a robin had one with the usual colours. Still, he thought of her, of her small white body, opening and closing her wings like a tiny angel come to earth.

IT was mostly fine to walk alone through his days. It was mostly fine, and then once in a while, it wasn't, and Henry longed for a friend to whom he could tell all his thoughts and feelings, all his secrets. Someone who would understand his emotions without him needing to explain them. He was always on the lookout for this friend, at the end of a forest path, around a stone wall, but there was never anyone there, no matter how much he looked, or even when he forgot to look. He began to think such a friendship was impossible for him, because while he may have been searching for this special friend, that friend seemed not to have been searching for him in return.

RECENTLY published, *Walden* was a more celebrated book than was *A Week on the Concord and Merrimack Rivers*. The new book was reviewed well, and Henry received several letters from admirers. One of them was from a man in his forties, Daniel, who wrote at length about his own efforts at building a shanty on a little piece of wilderness near his home in New Bedford. He wrote to Henry very familiarly, which came, Henry surmised, from thinking that he knew him from reading *Walden*. It was an odd feeling to be so intimately addressed by a stranger, and it was a bit unpleasant.

You have readers now, said Emerson. *Their presumption is forgivable. You wrote your book for them.*

But did I? thought Henry. When he was writing he wasn't thinking of anyone on the other end of the experience. It wasn't that he was writing for himself, because he did want people to read his book, but he was never thinking of them while he was doing the writing. It was more that he was having a relationship with the page itself. He laid down his line of words and the page rose up to meet them. That was the satisfaction in the experience, not this strange, rambling letter from Daniel in New Bedford.

HENRY had been ill for weeks and not able to go on his long walks. His legs felt unable to hold him up and his cough had returned. He grew his whiskers over his throat to help protect his lungs and lay in bed writing letters to his friends, asking them to come and visit, but everyone was busy.

Sophia climbed his attic staircase once or twice a day, bringing with her additions for the herbarium.

What's it like out there? he asked.

Hot.

That's not a good description.

Hot and humid, said Sophia. She showed him the bladder campion she'd picked. *I think there are people who make soup from the leaves,* she said. *Should we try it?*

Later that day she returned with a cup half full of green liquid and handed it to her brother.

As it happens, I didn't have enough leaves, she said. *They boil down quite quickly.*

Henry took a delicate sip from the lip of the cup.

It's a little bitter, he said.

Yes. It might only be something we would eat if there were nothing else to eat, said Sophia.

The Thoreau siblings had always been in accord. There had not been the competition between them that was evident in some other families. Instead, they had inspired one another, and each tried to further the ideas and exploits of the others. So, when Henry was ailing, Sophia took on all his interests in addition to her own. Many of those interests already overlapped, but she made sure that she botanized for more hours and that she experimented with what she found. All the while telling Henry everything.

HENRY was weak and ill for close to five months, barely able to walk sometimes. His overall condition had deteriorated, even though the doctor could find nothing specific that was wrong with him. He languished at home and was looked after by his family. Finally, the moment came when he had recovered enough to go outdoors again, although he still felt a bit fragile, a bit unsure. He made himself feel better by surveying the air temperature as he went about his July day.

It was ninety-three degrees on the north side of the Thoreau house. At his customary bathing place on the river, the temperature had dropped to eighty-eight degrees. When Henry took to the water to swim, he measured the water temperature in contrast to the air. Six feet from the shore and one foot deep, the water had dropped to eighty-four and a half degrees and only dropped three-quarters of a degree more when he was right in the middle of the river and completely submerged.

The next day the overall outdoor temperature had come down to eighty-six degrees. Henry walked along the rail tracks near Walden and measured the heat between the rails. It was 103 degrees. Then he rowed his boat out to the middle of the pond and recorded the air temperature there as being eighty degrees.

WHILE none of his close friends were available to visit, Henry's fan Daniel came to Concord without an invitation. Instead of being affronted by Daniel's impromptu visit, Henry was grateful for the company and they spent four days together. Daniel expressed great enthusiasm for Concord and invited Henry to come and see him in New Bedford. Henry went, a bit reluctantly, but found he was glad of the change of scenery when he arrived at Daniel's house. It was nice to be shown the woods by his children and to see Daniel's shanty. At night there was music in the parlour, and in the daytime there were excursions out into the countryside. When Henry returned home at the end of his time in New Bedford, he felt refreshed and finally had some of his old energy back. He never again had as much energy as before he was ill, but he had recovered enough to go back to walking and writing.

AT Walden Pond Henry met Alek shouldering his axe and striding through the woods. It was ten years since they first met, when Henry came to live at the pond. They sat together for a while on two stumps. Alek didn't know that Henry had been ill, which Henry found reassuring.

What news of the world? he asked.

Have you heard the rooster crowing in the woods? said Alek. *A whole cage of chickens fell from a cart, and they have been wandering around these woods for days, enjoying their freedom.*

Alek tapped his axe head on the ground between his feet.

Free eggs now perhaps? he said. *And you'd be the man to find them.*

More than once Alek had come upon Henry poking about in the undergrowth, or lying on his stomach on the ground, examining insects.

Henry loved that Alek, in answer to the question about the world, talked about the escaped chickens. He wondered if Alek even knew the real news of the world. And then he immediately thought that the runaway chickens were as real as any of the rest of it.

HENRY caught a screech owl. It was sitting on a stump, and he managed to come up behind it and grab it. First he wrapped it in a handkerchief and dropped it in his pocket, then once at home he put it into a box that he could cover and make into a cage. The owl was angry at the capture, hissing and snapping when Henry tried to reach into the box to touch it. He had wanted to survey the bird, but the owl had other ideas and dug a talon into Henry's hand so hard that he drew blood.

Henry kept the owl for a day, watching it and writing about it. When he took the owl back to where he had found it, the owl was reluctant to exit its box cage and had to be lifted out. Then it stood on the ground for a while, looking around in surprise, even though it was in the exact spot only twenty-four hours previous. Henry shook a stick at it, and it hopped onto a low branch of an evergreen, but still seemed perplexed. When he waved a stick at it again, the owl hopped to a slightly higher branch, and there Henry left it, sauntering away to eat wild apples as he walked, thinking about how the screech owl hated the box cage, but adapted to the prison so quickly and couldn't seem to recognize its freedom again.

DANIEL wrote asking Henry to come and visit him again, but Henry declined. There was something about the eagerness of his new friend that he found distasteful. Daniel seemed so willing to believe all of Henry's words and to follow every one of his actions, but what did Henry get from Daniel? This was perhaps not so easily answered.

IT was a new winter, and this one was not as cold as the last, but the snow kept falling and created huge drifts everywhere. Henry used snowshoes to walk through the woods and carried a stick that he used to measure the depth of the snow. He had carved lines into the wood of the stick at one-inch intervals, and he jammed the stick into the snow every ten steps.

Henry reasoned that the snow would be deeper in the woods, because the trees took up space there, thus forcing the snow higher, but there was actually less snow there when he measured. The trees themselves held snow in their branches, and so not as much of it had fallen on the ground beneath them. But just as he decided on this line of reasoning, it snowed again, and this time there was more in the woods than in the open fields, and Henry had to adjust his thinking again. The wind was to blame for this change. Snow, it seemed, was made variable by many differing circumstances.

THERE was a new cat in the Thoreau household called Min. She was still a kitten, although mostly grown. Her behaviour though was not the least bit adult. On this first day of February, she chased after Sophia's broom as Sophia swept the parlour, attacking the straw bristles and latching onto them, so that Sophia was sweeping the floor with the cat as much as the broom. When she tired of this game, Min raced around the room at top speed, narrowly missing crashing into furniture, then tore up two flights of stairs to the attic, where she threw herself out the open window, landing over twenty feet below in a snowdrift. She disappeared into the drift—neither Henry nor Sophia could find her when they dashed downstairs to look outside—but reappeared a few hours later in time for lunch, with no apparent harm having befallen her from the plunge or the snow.

IT continued to snow hard and Henry kept measuring the snow, and now that it was the middle of winter, he also measured the thickness of the ice on Walden Pond. At its thickest the ice was twenty-two and a half inches. The snow had a range of depths now that fresh snow had drifted onto the old snow and then was blown around every time there was a new storm. It was a constantly shifting, changing world, and his snow surveying just emphasized this point.

HENRY was not oblivious to the fact that while he was intent on studying nature, most of those around him were intent on destroying it. There were barely any coyotes or beavers or deer in the woods, as they had been hunted to the point of extinction. One neighbour shot foxes and sold their pelts. Another shot ducks for sport. Henry even met a man who killed only woodcocks and had shot so many that no one else had seen one around for years. One hunter after partridge surprised a hawk in the act of killing one, and the hunter took the partridge away from the hawk, as though he had killed it himself.

MIN the cat liked to sleep on the dough that Cynthia left out to rise for the morning bread. She was often found snoring in the midst of it while pillows of dough inflated all around her.

When she disappeared one February night and was still missing four nights later, everyone feared the worst. She might have got locked inside a barn, or eaten by foxes or roaming dogs. Most likely by now, she had frozen to death in the cold. Her antics, always annoying at the time, were suddenly missed and discussed with sentimental reverence.

The bread doesn't taste as good if the cat hasn't been lying on it first, said Cynthia, when the family was gathered around the breakfast table.

But Min returned as swiftly as she'd departed, slinking in the kitchen door one morning, her fur clumped together and her bones showing through her skin. The family surrounded her, feeding her chopped meat and warm milk, stroking her matted fur, trying to ascertain from her condition where she might have been.

Outside in the woods, said Henry.

Or trapped inside a shed, said Sophia.

She might have suffered a fit, said Aunt Louisa. *I had a cousin who suffered a bad fit and then couldn't remember anything about who she was.*

But Min remembers who she is, or else she wouldn't have come back home, said Sophia.

Wherever she had been, Min wasn't talking. She ate the delicate offerings with gusto and then curled under the kitchen stove to sleep the day away.

In May Henry took Emerson with him when he went to Sawmill Brook to look for a yellow violet. They hadn't been out botanizing together for some time, and Henry found that he had to explain a lot of what he was doing instead of Emerson naturally understanding. He realized with a start that although Emerson wrote a lot about nature, he wasn't actually out in it all that much.

The violet proved elusive, but Henry waded out into the brook to look at some bogbean. He had been keeping careful track of when various plants came into bloom, as he meant to make a kalendar for the environment around Concord.

It's been out approximately five days, he said to Emerson, after examining the bogbean.

Not six, said Emerson. *Or four and a half.*

But Henry had heard the song of a redstart and had left

the brook in search of the bird, spyglass in hand. Emerson was still smirking over the bogbean, and Henry had darted off after the redstart and found two grosbeaks and was now following the song of the mysterious night warbler that he had heard for years now, but had never been able to identify.

There you are, he said, when Emerson finally caught up. *You've missed so much.*

1855~1856

AFTER much asking, Henry finally took Daniel to see the site where his little house on Walden Pond used to stand. Each time he had returned to the spot, the depression in the ground was a little more overgrown and it was harder to distinguish the site as having once belonged to him, as having been a place where he had once lived.

But Daniel had arrived at the spot with a head full of ideas about what it was, and so he was not disappointed in the shallow pit filled with seedling trees and grass.

He paced out the dimensions of the house and stood for a long time at each of the corners.

It really was a modest affair, said Henry, embarrassed by the reverence. *I only lived in it for a little while.*

Yes, but you wrote the book there, said Daniel, moving to stand meaningfully by the remains of the fireplace.

Well, only some of it, said Henry. *I was writing another book most of the time.*

But Daniel was undeterred. His mythical Walden was a much more powerful dream than Henry's reality.

You lived here in complete solitude.

Actually, I often had visitors. And there were many passersby.

And there were others living in the wood—former slaves and some Irish families.

You revelled in the company of the birds and beasts.

It wasn't all halcyon, said Henry. *I was particularly bothered by one woodchuck who was eating through my bean field.*

Daniel had walked purposefully down to the shores of the pond and was gazing out over the water.

You swam here, he said.

Yes.

And drank the water.

Yes.

Daniel bent down and scooped a handful of water from the pond. He closed his eyes and brought the water slowly to his lips.

Nectar! he pronounced, so joyfully that Henry gave up trying to fight him and knelt down to drink beside his admirer.

HENRY went to visit Martha Simon. She was the last member of the Wampanoag tribe living in the area around New Bedford. He wanted to ask her to teach him her language.

The hut where she lived near the sea was smaller than his house on Walden Pond, and just as sparsely furnished. There was a little garden adjacent to it, containing mostly lettuce, and a huge drift of empty clamshells piled beside the garden. Martha returned from along the beach a little while after Henry arrived. She was older than he'd expected and sat listlessly opposite him while he peppered her with his prepared questions.

I don't know any language but English, she said, halfway through his explanation about who he was and what he wanted from her. *I've been with whites since I was seven.*

It was clear she did not want him pestering her, and viewed his curiosity and questions as just that. Henry felt discouraged, picking up his hat, readying to go. Inside the hat was the plant he had collected that morning, a stalklike flower with multiple white blooms. He knew it by its Latin name, *Aletris.*

Martha Simon saw the plant resting inside his hat. *That's husk-root,* she said. *You can use it to help a weak stomach.*

Henry wished now that he had brought along a whole hatful of plants to show Martha Simon.

BRONSON Alcott had been three times to see Walt Whitman at the farm of a friend north of New York City.

You must meet him, he said to Henry. *He is just like you.*

So, Henry travelled with Alcott one Saturday in November to meet the author of the new poetry collection *Leaves of Grass.*

He did not think the loud, coarse man like him at all. Whitman was big and broad, and his flesh was strangely red-coloured. He clapped Henry on the back and almost knocked him over, declaiming his poetry for too long after lunch, so that Henry grew restless and twitchy in his chair. The poems themselves, while purporting to be about nature, were so full of Whitman's presence that the nature receded over a distant hill and the listener was left with the striding *I, I, I* of the narrator taking up all the room in the landscape.

Do you really think I am like that? asked Henry on the return journey to Concord.

Well, quieter perhaps, but you both love the outdoors, said Alcott.

Henry was silent for much of the way home, mulling over what he had learned that day—not about the poet Whitman, but about his friend Bronson Alcott.

Mouse, said Sophia when she passed Henry on the stairs. Later she told him how Min had been playing with a mouse in the yard, batting it back and forth between her paws, when the neighbour's rooster came over to have a look at what she was doing. He immediately seized the mouse in one of his talons, tossed it into the air, and caught it in his mouth, swallowing it and then crowing in celebration.

And what of Min? asked Henry.

She didn't seem to mind. She can always find herself another mouse.

It was colder now. Winter was coming on, and Henry looked forward to the season of limitations, because it forced him to try new avenues, things he might not have considered in the more easeful months. He also looked forward to getting out his boat again come springtime. And it was always pleasing to think of the first flowers from deep inside the snowy vault of January. Part of the thrill of the seasons was in anticipating the changes the following season would bring.

WALKING by the river one day, Henry happened upon a servant girl lying face down, cutting a hole in the ice with a hatchet. She seemed exhausted, was flailing about and barely making a mark on the ice. Henry stood on the shore, watching her, and then called out to her.

The ice is thinner if you move upstream. Easier to cut a hole there.

The girl scrambled to her feet, gathered her skirts around her, and did as he said. He followed along from the bank to make sure she went to the right spot.

Where's your pail? he asked, for the girl only carried the hatchet.

My what?

Your pail. For the water. It was impossible to take water from the river without something to carry it in.

The hole is not for drinking, yelled the girl cheerfully. *It's to drown a cat in.*

↖

SOMETIMES Cynthia talked to her children about her past. One thing reminded her of another and she was down a path of story, often after supper, when they were all sitting in the parlour together.

Tonight she was remembering Cold Friday, which happened two years before Helen was born, when Cynthia was twenty-three.

The temperature dropped so sharply, she said, *that the water froze on the dishes as they were being washed. Ink froze in the pens when we tried to write, even if we were sitting right beside the fire.*

People dropped dead in their houses, and the animals perished in the barns.

Is it still the coldest day you remember? asked Henry. *Was it colder even than two years ago?*

The coldness of that winter had been remembered as the winter when only the cat dared venture outside, for which she was still considered heroic by all of them.

Yes, said Cynthia. *It was colder than two years ago. I think you'll find that others will agree, if you ask them.*

What was the worst thing? asked Sophia.

Why do you always want to know the worst thing? said Henry.

Because it's always the most interesting, said Sophia. *Much more interesting than the best thing.*

Well, there was no best thing, said Cynthia. *It was Cold Friday.*

The best thing might be the name, said Henry.

Sophia leaned forward in her chair. *The worst thing, Mother,* she said.

Cynthia frowned, trying to think of something to offer her youngest. This was often the trouble with telling her children anything about the past, especially these two—they always wanted a little more than she had to give. The story ended for her with the recounting of the details of the cold. She wasn't prepared to prioritize the details from best to worst.

The worst thing, she said, *is you asking me what the worst thing was.*

EMERSON's son, Eddy, made a snow cave. Henry walked over to see it. The cave had been built out of a snowdrift and had a small entrance that had to be crawled through, and then a larger, circular room, where Eddy had put a lantern and where one could sit up.

Emerson was away, for which Henry felt glad. He hadn't felt easy around his old friend since the day they went to look for the yellow violet. Anytime they were together, he felt the differences between them. It was better when it was just Lidian and the children—Eddy and Ellen—and himself.

First Eddy disappeared into the cave and tried calling out to see if those on the outside could hear him. His voice was so muffled that it sounded as though he was calling from two streets over.

Let me try, said Henry, when Eddy clambered out of the cave.

He was surprised to find that the interior of the cave wasn't very cold, that the lantern provided heat as well as light. Henry settled himself in the middle of the round room and started talking in a normal voice.

Can't hear you, yelled Eddy through the entrance hole.

Henry tried shouting, and his voice bounced back to him off the curved snow walls.

Was that better? he asked, when he crawled out.

Only slightly, said Ellen. *It was still not much more than a whisper.*

Lidian stood next to Henry, leaned over to him.

I think this is how I always feel, she said. *As though I'm yelling through a wall of snow and no one can hear me.*

Henry was startled at her confiding in him. Once, he and Lidian had been good friends. He had lived with her and the children while Emerson was in Europe, and they had talked every night after the children were abed. But it had been years since they had said more than a few words to each other. Henry thought that it must be hard to be married to the great man. Lidian had been Lydia when she married Emerson at the age of thirty-two, but he didn't like how her name sounded and changed it. He called her Lidian and she only ever called him Mr. Emerson.

I think that is my natural state as well, he said.

Next, they took the lantern out of the cave and bricked it up in a small cave of its own, to see how much light would leak through the snow. With over four inches of snow cover, there was still enough light from the lantern to read by.

The snow made the lantern light look hazy, as though it was shining through fog.

All the attitudes of water! Henry said to Lidian. *How miraculous they are.*

She gave him a look that he could only read as disappointment that he didn't want to ask her more about her state of mind, and then she, slowly, walked away from the cave and back towards the house.

HENRY and Emerson continued speaking to each other, recommending books, talking about the seasonal changes in the woods and world, but the friendship had changed for Henry. He could not bear to think less of Emerson than he once did, but it had already happened. Emerson had disappointed him with his talk of Nature but reluctance to physically engage with it, and he knew that he had disappointed Emerson with his lack of literary ambition.

Henry decided that the friendship was over on a cold day in February, and then, a few days later, a house that he had recently surveyed burnt to the ground. He went to stand among the sizzling, blackened timbers. He was, in fact, by accident, one of the first on the scene and saw the charred remains of the man who had lived there. It was not hard to think that one thing was the other, that the house of friendship with Emerson had burned to the ground, and all that was left were cinders and ash and the crisped bones of the former occupants.

There was a cat, said a small boy who was part of the crowd that was gathering. *I saw her run into the flames.*

There was no cat, said the man who stood beside the boy and was perhaps his father. *The cat was drowned long ago.*

All concern seemed to be for the phantom cat and none for the man whose body lay twisted up with the burnt beams and walls of his home.

EMERSON became ill with measles after returning from a lecture tour. There were a few days when his condition was dire and it was unclear if he would recover. He asked for Henry to come and see him.

Henry sat by his bedside and watched the bedclothes lift and fall with Emerson's breathing as he slept his fever away. The simple act of Emerson breathing made Henry feel better about their friendship. What happened when you were with someone was very different from what happened when you were thinking about them. Being physically near to Emerson when he was ill mended some of Henry's complaints of him.

Emerson recovered, and the friendship, while never as close as it once had been, was back on stable ground.

HENRY went to visit Daniel in New Bedford. They walked together on the shore and in the woods. Sometimes Henry went walking with Daniel's dog, Ranger, a big Newfoundland who courteously waited at each fork in the trail to see which route Henry preferred.

The men spent a lot of time together in Daniel's shanty, and as was Henry's wont, he surveyed it.

The shanty was barely any distance from Daniel's house, so close that it looked like a shed belonging to the main building rather than a separate entity. It was not built by Daniel, but was built for him, and was twelve feet by fourteen feet, with small windows on every side and a box stove and chimney on the wall opposite the door. The wood was specified by Daniel to be western cedar, but Henry noticed many boards from eastern trees in the mix. The shingled roof matched the colour of the walls, and there were shutters on the windows, painted a dark brown. Inside the shanty the wooden beams had been left open. There was no plaster on the walls.

The furniture was much the same as Henry had had in his little house on Walden Pond. There was a sofa and a table, some bookshelves and a place to stack wood for the stove. But Daniel had done something to the interior that Henry would never do. He had tacked up bits of paper everywhere with quotations written on them from books he had read and admired. (Henry was tempted to look for the pieces of paper with quotations from his own *Walden*, but he resisted). So, Daniel's writing space was filled with the words of other writers, every spare inch of wall covered with one quotation in English, another in Latin. Over the doorway was written, in Latin, the motto:

Fortune and Hope, a long adieu!
My ship is safe in port.
With me is nothing left to do,
Make other lives your sport.

WHILE at Daniel's they went to visit a young Irish woman who lived with her parents in a modest house, where she taught school.

Her father is a wastrel and her mother is high society, said Daniel, as they walked up the drive to the house. *A bad match. But you will like Kate.*

Henry did like Kate, much to his surprise. She was bold and strong, strode across the hall to shake his hand and then suggested they go outside to continue their visit.

I can't bear to be indoors, she said, falling into step beside Henry. *I can't breathe in there. I take my students outside as much as possible.*

I used to do that, said Henry. *When I had students.*

He snuck a look at her. She shone with good health and seemed twice as robust in body and spirit as he was.

I read your book, she said.

Which one?

Walden.

And did you like it?

The first part was a bit slow, but it picked up. She grinned at Henry.

Well, beginnings are hard, he said.

Are they? Kate grinned at him again, and Henry found himself blushing. They had walked on ahead of Daniel.

I mean to live as you do, she said. *When I've saved enough money, I will go back to the house where I was born, which is little more than a ruin now, and I will live there alone. I can farm and weave and know how to keep sheep and chickens, although I'm not so certain about how to shingle the roof.*

If you can do all those other things, the roof will be easy, said Henry. *It's just about keeping the tiles straight and working to a pattern.*

He had never met a woman like Kate, a woman so much like himself.

Perhaps you will visit me there? she said. *To make sure I'm keeping the tiles straight.*

DANIEL would not ever sleep in his shanty, even though it was so near to his house, because he was afraid of lightning and could not be alone if there was a storm. Henry had met dogs who were afraid of storms, but never a man. Daniel was also very afraid of death and wanted to live forever, could not bear to think that he wouldn't.

It would be easier on you perhaps if you could believe in some kind of a god, said Henry.

How can I believe in God if he created both lightning and death? said Daniel in reply.

Henry almost laughed, but could see that Daniel was seriously perturbed, so he turned his back and pretended to examine the bark of a pine tree to hide his amusement.

HENRY had a pair of corduroy trousers made for him. The material was a light grey colour. He had noticed, from the times he had walked around naked after bathing, that the animals were more inclined to come towards him if he wasn't wearing his black clothes. Now he had trousers the colour of clay and could wear a white shirt and none would fear him. Corduroy material was generally shunned by the elites of Concord, as it was worn by the Irish and thought to be for the clothes of those of a lower situation.

CYNTHIA talked of the sounds she used to hear at night when she was a young girl.

Cows lowing and night birds. Sometimes a drum beating far off in the distance.

What was the nicest sound? asked Sophia.

The neighbour whistling to his team of horses, said Cynthia. *He was a very good whistler and could carry many a tune. I think the horses enjoyed the whistling.*

They were sitting in the parlour after supper. The windows were open, and they could hear the creak of cartwheels on the road, the barking of a faraway dog. John Sr. was working in his pencil factory next door, as he did most evenings, trying to keep pace with the ever-increasing orders. The Thoreau pencil, with Henry's new design, was becoming the pencil of choice for Americans.

What I liked best, said Cynthia, *was to sit on the doorstep with the door open, facing into the darkness, and the only sound behind me was the ticking of the clock in the hallway of the house.*

1857~1858

I n 1856 an enslaved Black man named Dred Scott had sued the U.S. government on behalf of himself and his wife, Harriet. They had been taken from the slave-holding state of Missouri to Illinois, which was a free state. Scott argued that he and Harriet should now be free because of this, but in March 1857, the Supreme Court declared that people of African descent were never intended to be protected under the Constitution and were not, in fact, citizens, and therefore could not be citizens of any state, free or otherwise.

At the Thoreau breakfast table, this news, announced by John Sr., was greeted with stunned silence. If the free states weren't free at all for Black men and women, what then?

Henry thought of Helen and her conviction that the wrong of slavery would be righted by the work of the abolitionists. With this legal decision, things seemed to be moving backwards.

John Brown, the abolitionist, was coming to Concord to give a talk, and the Thoreaus immediately asked him to lunch with them.

Brown was a tall and slender man in his fifties, with an iron-grey beard and eyes of the palest blue. He was polite at the lunch table, pleasing and thanking like any genteel guest. But when John Sr. expressed his reservations about the violence that Brown was extolling in his fight to end slavery, Brown pounded his fist on the tablecloth.

I would rather a whole generation die the most violent deaths than slavery live for even one moment longer, he said.

HENRY was considering writing a book about the coastline of Cape Cod, and so he travelled there in June. He walked along the beach, marvelling at the many footprints in the sand, and the skeleton of a whale washed up on the shore. He tried to count a flock of gulls and lost track at one hundred, walked up Mount Ararat, spent time watching the fog roll in from the Atlantic.

He had been four times now to the cape and decided that was enough for him to be able to say something about it in print. He remembered what he had said to Kate—*Beginnings are hard.* It was because beginnings could be anything. He could begin with the footprints or the broken hull of whale bones or the fog. A beginning put you on a path to an ending, so it mattered where you started. But the beginning was also important because it had to be a place from where he wanted to continue on. The beginning had to mean something to Henry. Why put the words down otherwise?

Henry started his book with the story of the shipwreck of the Irish emigrants that he and Ellery chanced upon when they first came to the cape.

HENRY measured a buckthorn in the Yellow Birch Swamp, and later surveyed a new property for Bronson Alcott. The buckthorn was a full seventeen feet high with a circumference of one foot and ten inches. Alcott's new house had woodland and an apple orchard, with which the Alcotts hoped to raise their income. There were twelve acres that came with the house, and this is what Henry surveyed. The property was back in Concord, and the Alcotts would once again be neighbours of the Thoreaus, after their nine-year residency in Boston, for which everyone involved was grateful.

IN the spring Henry had bought some seeds for "large yellow squash," and then had watched, amused, as all through the summer, one of the squash just kept growing larger and larger. When he weighed it in September, it was 123 pounds and 8 ounces, which was roughly the same weight as himself. He entered it into the agricultural fair and won a prize, but when the man who bought the squash cut into it, the flesh was spongy and inedible.

It's little more than a weed, said Henry to Sophia afterwards.

It was an impressive weed, said Sophia.

I will never again buy seeds where "large" is the first word on the packet, said Henry.

He had felt a flush of pride when he won the prize for his squash, which made his disappointment at its failings doubly painful.

In autumn Henry climbed up to the top of Fairhaven Cliffs to look out over the valley of brightly coloured leaves. The red and yellow were looped through with the blue of the river. The red so rich in hue, but the yellow brighter and more visible from farther away. It was wholly peaceful and beautiful looking down at the autumnal tints, until Henry saw a small parade of black figures carrying a long box to the churchyard. A burial. Some family was one member poorer tonight at supper. Someone's brother perhaps, carried aloft on the shoulders of his friends.

In January Henry made a trip to the Natural History Rooms in Boston. There was only twenty miles between Concord and Boston, so the journey was easily made by rail. Henry liked to go to the Natural History Rooms whenever he had a question about nature that needed answering. On this visit he looked at a little grebe and a coot and a golden eagle, all dead, then at a live young bald eagle being kept in the cellars of the museum. By imitating the song of the night warbler for the professor who worked there, Henry finally had its identification confirmed as a white-throated sparrow, who apparently sang its tuneful flight of notes both day and night. While it was a relief to finally know what the bird was that had been puzzling him for years, it was always just a little disappointing when a mystery was solved.

A Chippewa doctor was to lecture in Concord one night near the end of winter, and Henry went to hear him. The man was dressed in tribal regalia and had brought various items with him to show the crowd—a blowgun, which he demonstrated by shooting an arrow into an apple, and a cradleboard that had notches on it to record the infant's age by the number of full moons, and which Dr. Maungwudaus put on his back to show how it was carried by a mother. Most of this felt like a performance to Henry, like the doctor was just giving the audience what they wanted from him. Henry could recognize this from his own performances, when he presented a lecture about one of his books.

Dr. Maungwudaus complained about having to speak English to the crowd, said he had to twist his jaws about to make the words. Then he went on to talk about his native language and how the words the Chippewa used for nature were to do with engagement. They were not the static descriptions that scientists used. In Henry's language there was one idea of *tree*, but in Dr. Maungwudaus's there were many. There was a word for a single oak tree, and a separate word for a grove of oaks, and another word for a tree that had been struck by lightning, and a term for an event that happened beside a tree. The English scientific terms were words for indoors, but the Chippewa language had been made and used outdoors. Henry had felt it before, on the ill-fated moose hunting trip, but now, on this March evening in Concord, he could see clearly how shoddy the language he existed within was for the natural world where he spent most of his time. How could he hope to describe what he felt and experienced using the inadequate language he was born into?

THE first bluebird was the line where winter crossed into spring. Often Henry heard the birds rather than saw them, as though their song arrived before they did and the little stir of notes was what set the snow to melting.

Spring was a long catalogue of what had returned. The bluebird was followed by the song sparrow, who was followed by the lark. Then there were the frogs, and the constant low hum of the bees as they awakened and drifted among the new flower heads.

Snipe, said Sophia, when she passed Henry on the landing.

Old news, he said. *I heard it yesterday.*

Even with all his attention, with his daily walks, with writing everything down, it was impossible to keep on top of spring. At a certain point it just raced ahead, and Henry was left stumbling behind, never able to catch up to what was blooming or fruiting or here on the wing. He used to be frustrated by this, but now that he was older, he just gave over to it when it happened. He was even a bit relieved when it did happen, when spring became a green furnace that burned through every hour.

WHEN Henry played his flute outdoors, he tried to insinuate the music into the landscape, as though the notes he released into the air were no different from birdsong or the murmur of the wind through the pines. He wanted his actions and himself to be as natural as any other part of the woods and ponds and meadows where he spent his time.

Whereas once he thought that it was necessary for a writer to have something monumental to say, now he no longer cared. A singular voice that rose above all other voices to declaim its truth didn't seem as important as the erasure of the individual voice in the chorus of nature's cacophony. It was the tone he wanted to get right now, not the words. And while he still wanted to write for readers, he no longer wanted the type of literary career that was cultivated by Emerson or Whitman. Fame seemed hollow to him when compared to the fullness of the forest.

FOR an hour Henry stood motionless in front of a small woodland pond filled with spring peepers. He was trying to understand their song, and to decide whether every frog had its own individual cadence or if the overall blend was the aim. In early April the peepers were the loudest constant in the landscape, a hum repeated later in spring in fainter form by the bees. Standing by the lip of the pond, as still as any rush or tree, Henry filled his ears with the sound of the frogs. He could think of no other concert where his attention would be so unrelentingly rapt.

Peepers, he said to Sophia when he found her on the road walking home.

First catkins, she said, opening her hand to show Henry the plump cylinders lying on her palm like fat caterpillars.

Spring has begun, said Henry as they walked up the steps to their front door.

Yes, said Sophia, turning the handle. *And we were there for it, right at the beginning.*

There was a map for the seasons and they had both learnt it by now. Henry would be forty-one this year and Sophia thirty-nine. They had lived long enough on the earth, and in Concord, to know what to expect when.

Later that night Henry was awakened by thunder and a cascade of rain on his attic roof. He sat up in bed and could see a wire of lightning sizzling down from the heavens onto a nearby field. It was the first lightning of the year and signalled to Henry that summer was on its way.

HENRY caught a peeper and took it home, where it did not peep. He kept it for a while in a jar of water, taking it out briefly to measure it (nine-tenths of an inch long) and then to measure how far it could jump (eighteen inches in one go), and then he returned it to its woodland pond, where its silence turned to song when it was back with its kind.

SOMEONE stole Henry's boat—not for the first time—and he spent an entire day tromping around looking for it. The difficult thing being, of course, that the stolen boat could be anywhere on the water, and Henry could only walk along the shore. He did not find the boat, but he did see and hear many frogs, and then a marsh hawk hunting frogs. Also geese and the first goldfinch, some black ducks and pine warblers. The sting of losing the boat was lessened by the abundance of wildlife that he spotted in his quest to find it.

A hummingbird flew into the Thoreau parlour, attracted by Sophia's cut flowers in a vase by the piano. Henry quickly closed all the open windows, and he and Sophia watched the tiny bird sampling the nectar from the flower heads, its wings beating furiously to keep it in place above the blooms.

Can you feel that? said Henry. *It makes a breeze!*

Look at the throat, said Sophia. *As brightly coloured as the flowers themselves.*

They stood together, as near to the hummingbird as they dared, but it didn't seem afraid of them, didn't even appear to notice them, so intent was it on dipping its long beak into the neck of the flowers.

When it had visited each one of the blooms in the bouquet, Henry opened the windows again and waved the bird out into the garden. They watched as it hovered between the flower beds, its speed and stillness a mesmerizing combination.

It's both bird and insect, said Sophia. *Closer to a dragonfly in some regards than to a swallow.*

It would be a much lonelier world, Henry thought, without Sophia there to share the hummingbird, the snipe, the catkins, and peepers.

HENRY's boat reappeared as mysteriously as it had disappeared, and he paddled out in it over the recently flooded meadows to see if he could identify the now-submerged meadow plants. He drifted around for a very agreeable afternoon, peering over the side of the boat at the blurry underwater flowers. He could see broom sedge and *Phalaris*, the grasses easier to recognize because of their height. How quickly the flood had transformed the meadow world into an undersea kingdom! It was thrilling to Henry when one thing became another. Change quickened his pulse, and he liked the feeling of having to flex his mind around the new conditions. It made his imagination race. He was like the hummingbird, he thought, leaning out over the side of his boat as it floated lazily over the flooded meadow—both slow and fast, seemingly doing nothing at all while his mind darted this way and that in search of the sweet and the bright.

1858

HENRY wanted to walk the entire White Mountain range, which would take two weeks or longer to do. He invited Edward Hoar to go with him, because Edward was a good botanizing companion. Edward decided to hire a horse and carriage to carry their belongings, as they meant to camp along the way. They set out from Concord on July 2, 1858.

At first Henry liked the ease of the carriage, but he became bothered that the horse was choosing their route rather than himself and Edward. The horse decided which bit of ground it wished to step on and which it wished to avoid. The horse required water, so they camped the first night on a low bit of land beside a river and near to a cemetery. They read the epitaphs and bathed in the river, but it was hot and close, and Henry found that he had low thoughts on that low bit of ground.

His thoughts improved the next day, when there was a view and he could stretch his mind and imagination to fill that space, to move outwards towards the distant horizon. The view was of the Merrimack River, its broadness and quiver of current lightening his heart and bringing back memories of his trip there with John nineteen years ago. He thought the river lower now than it was then, but it could be that he remembered it as fuller and swifter because he had glorified that time with his brother. He spent the early evening hours of the first day wandering along the edge, trying to identify the animal and bird tracks in the mud.

The horse continued to bother Henry. On the second night, when they were in their tent and trying to sleep, it pawed at the ground and whinnied. Every time they passed where it was tied to a birch tree, it jerked and thrashed.

It wants something from us, said Henry. *I think it might still be hungry.*

But I've allocated the food, said Edward. *There's only so much for each day. I thought it would graze.*

Hard to graze in a forest.

I suppose so.

They were quiet, listening to the horse complain through the tent walls. It drowned out all other sounds, the night birds and animals they might otherwise be hearing, the shush of the wind in the pines.

They climbed Red Hill, and Henry took note of fleabane and toadflax on the way up. At the top they made tea, having hauled water up for that purpose, but the result was perhaps not worth the effort, as it was windy at the top of the hill and it took ages for the fire to get hot enough to boil the water.

As the journey progressed, the mountains got increasingly more wild and uninhabited, the tracks approaching them more overgrown. Some of the peaks had snow on them, all were windy, and the views were always breathtaking, no matter how hard the climb.

In Tamworth, New Hampshire, they temporarily left the horse and carriage at the house of the man Edward was hiring to help carry their luggage. It seemed a good decision to trade the horse for a human being, especially one who was working for them. Henry had often felt that he and Edward were being ordered about by the needs of the horse.

The man, Matthew, had the skeleton of a bear in his living room.

A bear in the wild makes a sound like a woman who needs help, he said, which Henry found hard to imagine, though they listened for it all through the subsequent nights.

The biggest trek was up Mount Washington. They moved through layers of treeline, first spruce and yellow birch, then hemlock, beech, and canoe birch, and next through different species of maple, finally traversing through only fir trees until they reached the rock ledge at the base of the summit. Here they stayed the night in a shanty and were fed beef tongue by the coal miners who were there and had been paid to provide them with supper.

At the edge of the treeline, Henry found his first alpine plant, a sandwort. At the summit there was moss and sedge, which had created a little saddle of meadow on the bare flanks of rock.

The clouds were low enough to touch, and if they were to settle around the hikers, it would be easy to get lost and wander off the edge of the mountain.

Later, Henry sprained his ankle when he attempted to jump over a brook. The blackflies swarmed them, and blood dripped down his forehead and the back of his neck. The flies were kept away by the smoke from a fire, although some in his party preferred to wear a kind of mesh veil that made the swarthy men look like reluctant brides.

It rained. They descended the mountain through the layers of trees, now in reverse order—fir, maple, canoe birch, beech, hemlock, yellow birch, and spruce. Henry heard an ovenbird near the base of the mountain.

The rain continued and was present for part of each of the following days. If it rained when they were on a peak, it was impossible to see anything below, but when it was clear, they could see the whole of the White Mountain range from the top of Lafayette.

The sprained ankle slowed Henry down, and he spent less time walking up mountains and more time writing up his botanical notes in camp. When he returned home after two weeks and opened his notebook to show Sophia, he found squashed blackflies on every page.

EMERSON was going hunting with a group of philosophers, lawyers, and poets in the Adirondacks. He showed Henry his new shotgun.

It's double-barrelled. I can load shot in one chamber and place a ball in the other if I choose.

He put his foot up on a chair in his study and laid the shotgun over his thigh, running his hand slowly along the polished wooden stock.

Have you even fired a gun before? asked Henry.

The finest minds will be there, said Emerson. *We will hunt and fish all day and then, at night, there will be lectures and music. Stillman will paint. We will dine on what we have caught that day.*

You'll cook as well as hunt and philosophize?

Of course not. We are bringing cooks.

Emerson picked up his gun and pointed it towards the window.

I might shoot a bear or a catamount, he said. *Or perhaps a pair of wolves.*

Have you had a lesson in shooting? asked Henry, but his friend ignored the question again.

Well, I'm sure whatever you do shoot, you'll write a long poem about it afterwards, he said.

What did you catch on your camping trip? asked Emerson.

A sandwort.

Emerson snorted.

It was an alpine sandwort, said Henry. *Very difficult to find.*

HENRY rowed out to look at a grove of black willows that were growing on the shores of the river near the Fairhaven Cliffs. He got out and measured them, and then spent a while watching them from his boat. He liked the shape of a willow leaf, and liked too how willow trunks were sometimes ribbed and twisted from the rapid growth of the tree—a growth like flight. He wondered if he came out here for hours every day, would he be able to see that growth while it was happening? Once, he had read a novel by a Chinese author called *The Two Fair Cousins*, where the central character, Pe, spent his later life studying the beauty of a willow grove. Pe compared the eyebrows of his beloved with the shape of a willow leaf. The novel had been written eight hundred years ago, but Henry had no trouble imagining the woman Pe described, nor appreciating the passion the character of the book felt for his own willow grove. The willow translated well, he thought, through both time and language and culture.

IN August the fields filled with golden flowers and the air filled with golden birds. Henry found a goldfinch nest and marvelled at the pale white eggs he found there. This inspired him to take an inventory of the birds he had seen and heard in August, and he made a long list in his journal, beginning with the marsh hawk and ending with the nighthawk. In between were the sparrows and goldfinches, a robin and pine warbler, flicker and kingbird and chickadee.

For a week or two, Henry rowed on the pond in the company of the summer ducks. They got used to his presence and allowed him to get close to them, the human and ducks drifting around on the surface of the water together. But then his neighbour shot the ducks and fed them to another neighbour, who paid for their plump bodies to end up on her dinner plate.

Why, thought Henry, was his pleasure at their being alive less essential than the pleasure his neighbours took from the ducks being dead? Why was it easier to kill something than to leave it be?

MISS Pratt had seen the white bobolink in the middle of a large flock over the meadows, but when Henry went to look for it, he couldn't find it. He did see the flock, but there was no white bird folded within it. He went back to the same spot for three days, but had no luck. He also had no luck spotting the white barn swallow that John Flint's son tried to shoot many times and, eventually, did.

The white thing that Henry did manage to see was the first frost, which arrived well before summer's end and killed the last of the bright July flowers in the woods and fields.

EMERSON returned from his week in the Adirondack woods. He told Henry that everyone was very impressed with his new gun, and that he had shot a sandpiper and blasted apart ale bottles with some of the other intellectual campers after dinner.

We drank the ale first, of course, he said.

Of course.

They were walking in Emerson's garden, the light already fading although it was still quite early. Another sign that autumn had arrived.

No bears or catamounts or wolves then? said Henry.

Emerson was quiet for a moment.

The sandpiper was much more difficult to shoot than a bear would have been, he said. *Because it was so small. I had to be very precise with my aim.*

A September swim was always bittersweet, because there was no telling how many more swims would be possible before the cold weather set in. Henry put his head underwater when he was bathing in the river, and the muffled sound of the above-ground world could have been from any summer day. But when he surfaced, the sound he heard was the singing of the crickets rather than the singing of the birds.

M IST filled the early morning fields, and when it lifted, all the dried stalks of Queen Anne's lace were filled with spider-webs, each one slung towards the next, so that the whole field looked like an ocean with the shape and shimmer of the webs like waves.

When Henry returned from his morning walk, Sophia was in the garden, standing motionless near the late summer roses.

The hummingbird is here, she said, as Henry sidled up beside her.

Our drawing room hummingbird?

I think so. They're territorial, are they not?

Yes.

So, it must be the same one.

They stood together in the September sun, waiting for the little bird to fly across their vision.

There! Sophia pointed towards the house, and Henry saw the bright blur of wings hovering above the window ledge.

Perhaps it's trying to get back into the drawing room, he said. *Easier to overwinter with us than make the long flight back to South America.*

THE best way to experience autumn was to drift past it in a boat. Ellery and Henry paddled lazily downriver, marvelling at the reds and yellows of the maples and poplars along the banks. There were wild grapes hanging from their vines above the water, and all they had to do was position their boat underneath and then pick the grapes while seated. The fruit was so ripe that it just rolled off the vines, and in minutes they had filled the prow. The smell of the grapes was sweet and strong and cascaded over them as they continued downriver.

We have to remember this when winter comes, said Henry.

Perhaps winter comes precisely to be a space where we can remember this? suggested Ellery.

Henry appreciated Ellery's company and perspective on his outings, but he was also grimly aware these days that others regarded Ellery as a wastrel. His wife had left him and taken their four children, after years of waiting for Ellery to settle into a profession and earn money to support his family. Ellery's desire for wandering was judged harshly by the citizens of Concord, while Henry's was tolerated because he was unmarried and without children.

A boy came to the door of the Thoreau house, bringing Henry an injured bird.

Cat got it, he said, passing over the parcel of feathers.

The bird pecked weakly at Henry, then lay motionless between his cupped hands as he took it upstairs to his attic room. He put it down on the floor and watched it hop along the boards. The bird was a rail, its big feet and heavy beak making it look a bit like a chicken. There was no blood on it and the feathers seemed intact. Perhaps it was mauled by the cat and just needed to recover?

Henry watched the rail for a while and then lifted it up and put it on the window ledge, so that it could see the outside world and be reminded that it wanted to return there. He remembered how quickly the screech owl he once caught became accustomed to its prison.

But mind when you go, he said to the bird, *that you stay well away from that house over there. The owner has shot a sandpiper, and he might be after trying his luck at a rail.*

H<small>ENRY</small> walked to the cliffs and watched the sun drop down over the last of the autumnal tinted leaves. Many of the trees were bare already, and all the apples had been harvested and packed away in cellars, or stored in buckets down the well, where the cool and dark would keep them fresher for longer.

Henry looked out at the tops of the trees, the distant blue button that was Walden Pond, then up at a pair of hawks who were circling on the air currents. Every time they spiralled higher, he could see the flash of light from the setting sun on the underneath of their wings. It was as though the colour of the leaves below had ascended towards the heavens, was rising higher and higher into the darkening sky.

AFTER a bout of solitary tromping, Henry desired company and decided to call on Ellery and see if he wanted to walk with him. As he strolled towards Ellery's house, he was thinking of his friend in the best possible way, to counteract the talk about Ellery that existed in town. Indeed, he had an idealized view of each one of his friends, formed perhaps when he initially met them and they seemed godlike and mysterious to him.

After Ellen and the children left him, Ellery moved into a small house on the main street of Concord. Henry knocked on the door, but no one came to answer.

Henry! It was Ellery's head, poking out of the upstairs window.

Will you come out walking? asked Henry.

I have a cold. It's best that I remain indoors for now.

Like a turtle going back into its shell, Ellery's head pulled back into his bedroom and he disappeared from view.

The idealized Ellery was always delightful and game for anything, but the real Ellery babied himself unnecessarily. Henry walked away from the house, annoyed and disappointed. He sometimes preferred his friends when they were absent. Was it perhaps the same for them in their friendships with him?

AFTER the first frost the apples that remained on the trees turned brown and started to dissolve into themselves. The crickets still played their raspy violins, but not in the evenings anymore, only in the waning heat of afternoon. The leaves of the red maple carpeted the earth, and the summer birds had flown. Meadowsweet was yellow and the poplar still held its leaves. The tap of the woodpecker replaced the summer bird-song, and the winds had started to blow cold through the pines. Lichens and mosses were now as visible as the leaves had been in summer.

Daniel, who also seemed to be cataloguing the changes in the season, sent Henry a packet of leaves he had collected from several trees, including beech, linden, walnut, and chestnut. Some of the leaves had dried and broken on their journey through the postal system, but it was nice to think of Daniel going about his day, doing much the same things as Henry was doing in his day.

HENRY found what he thought was a white-throated spar-row's egg in Emerson's garden. He made the trip to the Natural History Rooms in Boston to ascertain his find by matching it to the bird's egg collection there.

His egg did not belong to the white-throated sparrow. Nor did it seem to belong to any other bird. And, looking through the collection, Henry found that his hermit thrush egg actually was the egg of a Townsend's solitaire, and that the rail egg he found in Concord did not belong to either the Virginia rail or the clapper rail. It was perhaps the egg of a sora rail, but there was no corresponding egg in the Boston collection.

The Natural History Rooms, instead of clarifying things, had just made them all the more confusing.

John Brown and his band of vigilante soldiers had been fighting pro-slavery forces in Kansas, including murdering five unarmed men and boys, whom they had dragged from their homes in the middle of the night. Now Brown was moving his fight to Virginia. Some men in the north, including a reverend in Concord, were leaving their homes and families to go south to fight with Brown. But there were many who disagreed with his extreme violence.

Henry wished sometimes that he could be a man who would stride off into battle like that, but he knew that he was too peaceable a soul for that kind of fight. His strength was his observations and his words. The best he could do was to string a line of moments together and hope that they glittered and shone.

A neighbour told Henry about a runaway pig that had been on its way to the abattoir but managed to escape from the rail car and take to the woods. It was chased by both men and dogs, but the pig, being three hundred pounds and unafraid, turned and chased its pursuers instead, injuring a dog so badly that it had to be carried home by its owner. The next day more men were enlisted to track the pig, but again the pig turned on them and flipped one of the men onto his back by running between his legs.

At last account, said the neighbour, *the pig was holed up inside a barn and no one dared to enter.*

WINTER arrived via an overnight ice storm, although when Henry went out the next day to examine the world, the ice was already melting. Each glassy twig was dripping, and while the enrobed branches still clinked and tinkled like bells, that motion broke the coating and it fell to earth in a shower of crystal fragments. Nevertheless, it was always a thrill to see the world transformed, whether through ice or rain or wind. The change created possibilities where none previously existed, and that, to Henry, always seemed a positive development.

1858~1859

THE family gathered for Christmas in the Thoreau house. Aunt Jane, who was born on Christmas Day, liked to mention this every year.

My parents always said I was their favourite Christmas present.

But tell the part about the spoons, said Henry's father. His five sisters were all younger than him, but sometimes in their presence, he was the one who seemed a child again.

Oh yes, the spoons, said Aunt Jane. *My aunt Hannah was made so nervous by the event of my birth that, when she was doing the washing up, she threw all the spoons out onto the front lawn with the dishwater.*

John Sr. laughed uproariously, even though he had heard this same story every Christmas of his life.

Does it get funnier? Henry whispered to Sophia.

I think it gets less funny, she whispered back to him.

But later, after dinner, Henry thought that the annual reciting of the story of Aunt Jane's birth was not about how mirthful a story it was. For his father, the story was part of what told him who he was, and the telling of it reassured him that he was, indeed, this person—a person who found a nervous woman accidentally tossing silver spoons into the Christmas snow hilarious.

This was, in fact, the last time he would hear this story, and the last Christmas for John Sr. He had a fever soon after the holiday and took to his bed on January 13, dying there a few weeks later on February 3 of consumption.

He had been weak and coughing for the past year or two, but this had not interfered with his ability to enjoy life. He worked in the garden, walked to the post office to read the newspapers, noted the comings and goings of the Concord inhabitants. He was older, at seventy-two, than most of the town residents, had already outlived many of his friends and contemporaries. Consumption, which was no stranger to the Thoreau family, was the leading cause of death in the towns and villages around Boston.

Still, his death, when it came, was shocking, as all death is in the midst of life. Even though his death was so peaceful, it was still shocking.

Henry, Sophia, Cynthia, and the aunts had gathered around his bedside. It was a Thursday afternoon. The light slanted in at the window. John Sr. had not spoken for two days and not opened his eyes since yesterday morning. He was getting down to the business of dying, each breath a knotted cord he drew slowly into his lungs, his bony chest rising and falling under the bedclothes.

No one cried. It was somehow not sad at this moment, because he was dying so well. There was no suffering. Cynthia held one of his hands and Aunt Jane held the other. Sophia and Henry sat together near their father's head. All of them were watching him breathe and yet, when he stopped breathing, it seemed so surprising.

Henry, said his mother, *could you check to see if his heart is still beating?*

Henry laid his head on his father's chest. It was warm there, and he could hear, every so often, a faint and muffled thump.

His heart is still going.

John had stopped breathing, but his heart was still beating, so there seemed no point at which he had actually died, as he was both alive and dead at the same time. His lips and the tips of his ears began to turn blue, but each time Henry laid his head on his father's chest, he could still hear the slow knock of his heart in its cave.

It took a full two hours for John's heart to stop. Afterwards Henry couldn't understand why he was flooded with happiness, but he realized later it was because he had rested his head on his father's body, over and over again—something he had not done since he was a young child.

Two days later, out in the woods, Henry noticed that the birds did not sound as sweet as usual. He found no comfort in the changing weather or light, but was reassured by the constancy of the lichen on the bark of the trees and the surface of the rocks. Lichen never withered and died. It continued, through all weather and season, year after year, growing slowly outward, and always in contact with the skin of the trees or the stones. If Henry was younger, he would make the study of lichens his work. But it was enough, in these days after his father had died, to spend some time in the company of the lichen, to relish their fresh green colour after a winter rain, to admire their persistence, their vigour, their eternalness.

THE ice became too soft for skating, but Henry could still find some shady spots where the ice was hard—on the north side of a marsh, or in the shadow of a wooded hillside. One day, skating near the edge of a large pond, he saw, farther along the shore, a man and woman skating together. They circled each other, moving apart and coming together again, like the pair of hawks that drifted together on the air currents above Fairhaven Cliffs.

The sight of the pair filled Henry with loneliness, but in the next moment, he heard the familiar song of the blue-bird and watched as a small flock of them flew over the pond, returning from their winter home to live their summer lives in Concord once again.

Bluebirds were not the first birds to return this year. Blackbirds were recently spotted, and it seemed that the rob-ins had already been in Concord a week, although Henry had yet to see one. The birds were returning early this year, and it seemed no accident that their arrival had followed so swiftly on his father's death. One thing begat the other, or one thing helped ease the other. With the return of the bluebirds, Henry could once again appreciate the sweetness of their song.

The February bluebirds over the skating pond seemed not to have continued on to Concord, though, for Ellery reported his first bluebird there on March 7, and Emerson told Henry of seeing his first two days later. When Henry checked with Edmund Hosmer on his farm, he also said that he saw his first bluebird in that early week of March. So, it felt like some kind of blessing that Henry saw that little flock of bluebirds fly over him in the same month as his father had died.

THE snipe made its shuddery cry at twilight now that spring was creeping on. Using his breath, Henry could do a good imitation of the bird and practised it on Sophia by standing in the garden while she leaned out of his attic window. He ducked down behind a bush and took a great lungful of air before whinnying it out again.

How was that? he called up to his sister.

Is Mr. Snipe talking to me? she said, leaning out over the sill. *How marvellous! First he serenades me, and now he wishes to have a conversation!*

It seemed to Henry that half the people in Concord did not know what made the sound of the snipe. What was even more surprising was that most of those did not seem to care whether they found out or not. The ghostly twilight call could, in fact, be a ghost for all they knew of it. This was just another example, for Henry, of how his life was so different from the lives of his fellow citizens.

SOMETIMES Henry tired of the base categories for the four seasons. There were so many subtle changes that occurred in nature that one could divide the year up into many smaller seasons, some lasting only a number of days. He had started to do this for himself and noted today that they had entered what he called *the brown season*, which happened in the days between the last snow and the last frost. In this interval the world was all mud and decaying plant matter, all of it various shades of brown. After this short season would come the season of the willow, as the willow catkins were usually one of the first plants to bloom, and the shining willow leaf was one of the first leaves to emerge and one that was instantly noticed in the landscape.

HENRY sat on a white pine stump and listened to the song of the pine warbler in the forest. The song was light and airy, and then beneath it, as though accompanying the bird, there was the sound of two branches rubbing together, the vibrato sounding exactly like a viol. Henry never tired of the music of nature. So many songs going on simultaneously, one supporting another. All one had to do was find an old stump and sit down to listen.

HENRY hired a local man to help him with the survey for a woodlot in Acton. All day, while they were setting the line, Stedman boasted of all the birds he had recently killed.

I shot some crossbills who were opening pine cones, he said. *And an eider duck and four kinds of teal ones.*

I didn't know there were four kinds of teal ducks, said Henry. *Well, perhaps not anymore. I have shot so many.*

Stedman had killed grey ducks, black ducks, a whole flock of small white ducks that were two-thirds the size of a pigeon.

Shot most of those on the wing, he said proudly.

That evening, after supper, Henry went round to Emerson's to see Edward's aquarium. He had to peer closely at the glass container, as all the water creatures in it were so tiny.

There are two minnows from the brook, said Eddy. *And some larvae. I think they're dragonfly larvae.* He pointed to a faint shape floating on top of the water. It looked like a small twig husk. So impossible to think that one thing would become the other. Henry put a hand lightly on the boy's shoulder.

Thank you very much, he said. The dragonfly larvae proved enough to cancel out the catalogue of duck kills that he'd had to endure listening to today.

IN the summer Henry and Ellery made a trip along the Concord in Henry's boat. They didn't sleep on the boat, or even beside the boat in a tent at night, but instead walked back to their houses, or spent the night in the houses of acquaintances along the route, returning to the boat to continue with the trip each morning.

This was how age was measured, thought Henry, as they walked in the early morning along Corner Road. By doing the same thing twenty years apart, he could gauge the differences in himself.

The voyage with John was all about staying with the boat, being one with the boat, all of them flexing downstream with the current. But now the river was just part of everything, not central to it. Walking along the road in the early morning, Henry noticed the fog under the apple trees, the spiderwebs coating the grasses. In the evenings he walked home listening to the click and whir of the insects in the meadows.

While they were sailing on the river, Henry leaned over the side and looked at the ripples in the water, or at the lily pads—each one bigger than the span of his hand—that they drifted past.

They drank the river water, warm and muddy, out of an old clamshell that they kept on board for this purpose. They saw a blue heron and a number of small green bitterns, also a wren that was unfamiliar to Henry.

They talked and were silent in equal measure. When he was feeling his happiest, Henry sang his favourite song, "Tom Bowling," the sad lament about a young sailor who lost his life.

No more he'll hear the tempest howling
For death has broached him to.
His form was of the manliest beauty,
His heart was kind and soft;
Faithful below, Tom did his duty
And now he's gone aloft.

On the last day of their sixteen-mile trip, they sailed past a trailing parade of cardinal flowers, the stutter of red along the banks as deep and rich as arterial blood.

It had been the same river, but nothing about the trip felt like Henry's voyage with John. It might be, he thought, that while it was the same river, he himself had become a completely different person in the intervening years.

1859~1860

Now that John Sr. had died, Henry inherited the pencil factory and responsibility for the business. Some of this was pleasurable—walking through the woods in Acton, looking for a stone large enough and flat enough to use for grinding the plumbago for the pencils. But he resented having to visit the factory to inspect the goings-on, even though it was right next to the Thoreau house. In the factory the air was thick with lead and irritated his already weak lungs, so that one afternoon of visiting yielded three successive days of coughing.

Added to the annoyance of being in sole charge of his father's factory, was the fact of the army coming to perform muster in Concord in the early days of September. Their constant marching produced so much dust that the entire town was coated in it. Every surface inside the Thoreau house was covered in a film of white dust raised by the continual stomping of the soldiers' boots.

In September there was the annual cattle show in Concord. Every year was much the same as the previous year, with cattle and horses, pigs and poultry on display. There was the annual plowing match, a demonstration of working oxen, and a parade with music and speeches at the end by the Reverend Stebbins, who worked hard to combine both morality and farming in his oration.

Henry avoided all of that, as he had every year, but he did like to wander around the cattle show and look at the animals, and at the different fruits and vegetables. He liked to see the plentitude. The mounds of apples and carrots filled him with happiness.

This year he was most impressed with two varieties of apples—the Lady and the Maiden's Blush—each having one side of the fruit one colour and a different colour shading the opposite side. He was also taken with the largest apple there, a variety called Pumpkin Sweet. These apples were tall and almost rectangular, and each one seemed to weigh close to a pound when he held it in his hand.

HENRY went to the cliffs to look for acorns under the big oaks there. He wanted to plant the acorns and grow other oaks to help replenish the forest, as so many of the trees were being cut down.

It was hard to find an intact acorn, as the squirrels had been at them already, chewing through the outer layer to the seed within, or spiriting them away to store for the cold winter months.

The climb to the tops of the cliffs was a little harder than usual, a fact that Henry registered and then dismissed. Once at the summit he stood near the edge, catching his breath and looking out over the familiar view of trees, houses, and water. How many times had he climbed up to this view? And how many more times would he do it before his life was over?

THIS October there was a second spring. Plants bloomed again and the days were warm for a stretch, before becoming permanently colder. The migrating birds sang as sweetly as they left Concord as they did when they arrived there six months previously. Branches were loaded with buds in advance of spring. It was perhaps the sweetest time of year, because it both remembered and anticipated in the same moment. Much poetry had been written to spring, but this October spring was poetry itself.

HENRY made a list of all the fruits still on the trees and shrubs and vines, and comparing it to his list of five years ago, he found that there was more fruit at this time of year in 1854. Did this shorter fruiting season presage an early and cold winter? He recorded all of these details of the natural world in his journal, but it was hard to know if they meant anything beyond the fact of themselves. Still, he could not stop himself from recording the changes around him. It had become a compulsion, and as all compulsions were, it was a comfort.

The birch trees and ash trees were now bare of leaves. The leaves of the bayberry had fallen and the berries were all gone.

The chickadees sang louder and more often now that the birds of summer had fled. Apples cobbled the ground in the fields. And all around, with the morning frost and the evening chill, were the congregants of winter, already stiffening into place for the months ahead.

Did you hear that John Brown has been hanged? said the post-master. *He dieth as the fool dieth.*

All day Henry turned over this remark in his mind. He felt there was nothing foolish in the death of the abolitionist, hastily tried for treason after his failed attempt to arm slaves at Harpers Ferry in Virginia. Brown had believed that the only way to end slavery was through slave rebellion, because all peaceful means had amounted to nothing. He was not afraid to lay down his life in the name of abolishing slavery, and now that his life had indeed ended, he was being remembered as a madman by Henry's neighbours in Concord. They did not hesitate to call him insane or proclaim that it *served him right* to be hanged for his beliefs.

Henry remembered the day Brown had come to lunch at the Thoreau house. After lunch Emerson had dropped by with his children, and Brown had talked with Eddy about the need to cherish the individual, be they woman or man, Black or white. *Even animals*, he had said, *are unique to themselves. Give me a flock of fifty sheep and, after a day, I would be able to tell them all apart.*

Henry could not stop thinking about John Brown and the hypocrisy of those who pretended to support his cause but, in reality, were happy to see him hang. He railed against the injustice in his journal, and to whoever would lend him a sympathetic ear. But when he walked about in the world, the plants and animals had not noticed a change, did not give his human dilemmas a thought. The grebe still dove into the river, while the goldfinches flitted above it, eating the last seeds from the goldenrod along the banks. The moss glowed green in the hollows, and the scales of the lichen were silver upon the branch. The musquash swam in the pond, while the minnows darted beneath and the duck flew overhead. The trees were patient with their growing.

As more and more homes and buildings were constructed, more forests were cut down. A huge wood of oak and pine just outside Concord fell to the woodchopper's axe. Henry counted the rings in the stumps left behind and discovered from doing so that many of the trees were over a hundred years old. Each time a wood was destroyed, all the creatures in it also disappeared. Now it was rare to hear the song of an owl at night.

After years of not seeing Alek, Henry heard news of him this autumn. The woodchopper apparently lived in Lincoln, in a shanty he built himself, and he lived as simply as possible.

I heard that he only drinks checkerberry tea, said one of Henry's neighbours. *And little else.*

Henry thought back to his time at Walden and wondered if Alek had been influenced by him, as Henry himself was influenced by Charles and his shanty at Flint's Pond. Perhaps there would be someone who would take Alek as an example, and the simple shanty-dwelling life would ripple out into the future? It pleased Henry to think about this, to think that there might always be a person or two who desired to live simply and deliberately, in the heart of nature.

WALDEN Pond was shrouded in mist. The mist made the familiar strange. It blurred the shapes along the shore, obscured the trees, and hid the far end of the pond from view. How quickly did a landscape change from the known to the unknown? Henry once would have declared that he knew this place more intimately than any on earth, but now the black shapes twisting out of the fog did not resemble the trees he once gazed at for hours at a time. Stumps were recognizable by their shape, but the trees, the trees might as well have been creatures from another world, reaching their hooks out into this world.

IN early winter Henry went to Cambridge to look at *Gerard's Herball* in the Harvard library. He read through the descriptions of the flowers. They were not dry as scientific descriptions often were, but were almost exhaustively descriptive, full of Gerard's keen interest in their being.

Of the cattail, Gerard offered a breathless sentence: *Cat's Tail hath long and flaggy leaves, full of a spongeous matter, or pith, among which leaves groweth up a long smooth naked stalk, without knot, fashioned like a spear, of a fine and solid substance, having at the top a brown knop or ear, soft, thick and smooth, seeming to be nothing else but a deal of flocks thick set and thrust together, which being ripe turneth into a down, and is carried away with the wind.*

Gerard published his *Herball* at the end of the sixteenth century, over 250 years ago, and his descriptions still felt apt, but Henry thought of all that he had missed. There was much more to any plant than a simple description of its parts and colour, of when it bloomed and when it withered. An observer could spend an entire lifetime looking only at one particular flower and still not know very much about it at all.

HENRY and Ellery walked out together into winter and immediately had a disagreement because Ellery preferred to walk along the road rather than in the woods, where Henry wanted to roam.

Does it really matter if I go by road or wood? Ellery said. *Isn't it that we are out that is the important thing? Couldn't you be walking right now in a city as happily as you are walking here?*

Of course not, said Henry. *When I walk in the woods, I am making my own track. If you walk in the road, you are following a route laid down by others.*

It's just easier, said Ellery. *On account of the depth of the snow and the height of my boots.*

They walked along in silence, one in the road and the other at the edge of it, weaving in and out of the line of trees. Henry looked up at one point and saw the nest of the fiery hangbird, drooping down like a small basket from the end of a branch. He remembered the orange breast of the bird in spring and the sweet lilt of its song, but didn't mention the nest to Ellery, as he was still annoyed with him.

But when they got to Mill Brook and stared into the water there, Ellery pointed out the ripples on the sand along the bottom of the brook.

In Persia they call those marks chains, he said, *because of the wavy lines they make.* And Henry, glad to know this information, forgot his annoyance at his friend.

At Flint's Pond there were three fishermen dangling their hopeful lines through holes in the ice and giving lots of excuses as to why they hadn't caught anything.

This spot worked fine the other day, said one. *Not sure why it's not working today.*

The fish must have moved on, said another. *They do that, you know. Always on the move.*

But Henry didn't care about the fishermen's excuses or their lack of fish. His eye was caught by the yellow colour of the rushes on the opposite bank. How they were so subtle in summer that he never noticed them, but now in winter they had a warm and vibrant hue.

He was also struck by how tall the blueberry bush was on the little island in the middle of the pond that he called Sassafras Island.

It must be ten feet tall, he said to Ellery. *How could I have not noticed that before?*

Winter created a sort of blank background against which plants with the slightest bit of colour stood out. It was like seeing with a different set of eyes. The stars of winter weren't the bright, showy flowers of summer, but were what had been made invisible by all that colour—the pale gold of the rushes, the delicate basket of the hangbird's nest, the upright branches of the highbush blueberry, the *chains* in the sand on the bottom of the brook.

ON Christmas Eve, when most people were sitting by the fire in their houses, having a cup of cheer, Henry went back to Flint's Pond to measure the gigantic blueberry bush. He walked over the ice to the little island with his length of measuring tape. The five stems of the bush were united as one near the ground, and this thick trunk was thirty-one inches around. Three feet up, the trunk had divided into the five distinct branches, each of them measuring, on average, nine and a half inches in circumference.

Where the stems divided, Henry was able to climb up into the blueberry bush and sit there for a while. If it had been summer and the berries were ripe, he could imagine dining there, as though the blueberry bush were the finest restaurant in the land.

From his perch in the blueberry bush, Henry could see out over the ice of Flint's Pond. He could make out the tracks of a partridge near the shore. Perhaps the bird was a frequent visitor to the blueberry bush in summer and had decided to venture out, as Henry had, to see what was going on there at the end of December?

On Boxing Day Henry went skating, but his pleasure was dampened by the sight of a man with a gun, who was systematically breaking into the dens of the musquash—as many as twenty or thirty—to shoot the inhabitants inside. The ice was streaked red with their blood. For their corpses this hunter would get ninepence apiece, and the poor musquashes would be scraped and flayed and turned into winter hats.

On Fair Haven Pond Henry watched the wind scour the snow, creating ridges and then smoothing them out again. He watched a hungry fox walking around the edge of the pond, searching in the dried rushes and scratching at the rind of snow in the hopes of finding a winter meal of mouse or vole.

The fox had black tips on its tail and paws, stood tall and lean on its long legs. The soft way it moved made it seem aristocratic to Henry, a creature much more noble somehow than the common dog. He watched it through his spyglass, mesmerized by the grace and elegance of its hunger.

It was not just a fox's tracks in the snow that were recognizable to Henry, but his friends' and neighbours' as well. One man didn't lift his feet very high and seemed to slide along on his boots, so his tracks were indistinct and resembled the grooves made by the runners of a sleigh. Another man was always accompanied by his dog, so it was easy to tell where he had been walking, as the dog's prints weaved in and out of the man's. In darkness Henry could recognize the voice of one neighbour from half a mile away. Another he could tell from the slouch in his stride, the way one shoulder hung down lower than the other, when the man was but a coated figure walking in the road up ahead.

But who was watching him? Henry thought. Was there anyone out there who would recognize his tread in the snow, his voice in the night air, the particular angle of his body as he walked alone through the pine woods?

1860~1861

In winter the earth disappeared, and this is what made the season seem like it was another world entirely. The earth, which in springtime was the mud and muck that supported the teeming amphibious life, was entirely absent, buried beneath the snow and ice. In February, with the stronger sun, the ice appeared blue, and it was as though it had become the sky and Henry was walking across the blue of the heavens when he set out for the day.

Sometimes winter had come upon the world so suddenly that pieces of summer remained trapped within it—the gold rushes on the rim of the pond, green leaflets of clover frozen into the meadow snow. And just when Henry had started to think of winter as a kind of afterlife, as a mausoleum, into this still, white chamber flew the first robin or bluebird, pulling the bright chain of spring behind it.

There was a new book, just published in London earlier in the year, that was making the rounds among Henry's friends. *On the Origin of Species* by Charles Darwin purported an idea of *natural selection*, where animals and plants survived based on how well they could adapt and reproduce. The evolution of all species, including man, was based on this principle. In Darwin's theory God did not create the world, or a hierarchy where man was ranked above all the other creatures. Darwin's proposal was that man had actually evolved from the animals.

Henry read the book out loud with Bronson Alcott and two of his friends. It felt too important a book to read alone, as it required so much discussion. Everything in it was the opposite of what they had always been told to believe.

Afterwards, Henry walked home through the late afternoon winter air. He walked with a lightness in his step and the cold on his face unnoticeable. This was a momentous day. What he had always felt—that everything in nature was undeniably connected—had now become scientific theory.

THE ice retreated from the open meadow areas first, where the sun had easy reach. The ponds in the woods held on to their ice for longer, and the breakup was slow. First there was a little rim of melt around the edge of the pond, then a softening and sagging of the ice in the middle, and finally the sheet of ice divided into small islands, then little pieces that clinked against one another in the breeze. When the pond had enough open water to have ripples, then the first song sparrow was often seen. After the song sparrow came the first catkin.

It's all beginning again, said Henry, when he passed Sophia in the hallway before dinner.

Later they walked out together into the garden and stood in the patch of sunlight on the upper lawn.

Edward has already heard the first bluebird, said Henry.

Edward often hears the first bluebird, said Sophia. *His bluebird must be the swiftest of all the bluebirds, making the trip to his house weeks ahead of ours.*

They both looked towards the back door of the house, where John's bluebird box still hung, a little dishevelled, from its perch in the poplar.

We have to face the sad truth, said Sophia. *We have a very slow bluebird.*

Perhaps we have an old bluebird, said Henry.

Slow and old. And possibly also with a poor sense of direction.

A fire burned through a nearby wood just as the leaves on the trees were starting to come out—the fire racing through the forest faster than spring could arrive.

Henry walked through the char and smoke the following day, remembering the fire he and Edward had accidentally started when they were trying to cook a fish for lunch. That wood was mostly pine. This one was largely deciduous. Some of the smaller trees still held their first leaves, the bright green of new life shining like a star up ahead on the path.

But the fire was just one day in the life of Nature. It was one terrible day, but the next day the purple finches arrived and sang sweetly in the branches of the trees that were still standing, and they didn't seem to notice the remnants of the fire at all.

THE man Henry hired to help him with a survey of swampland told Henry a story about a nest of snakes.

They were found in a soft spot of ground where once was buried a horse, he said. *A great ball of snakes, striped and black and all twisted together. We killed them and laid their bodies out in a line and measured them. Three hundred feet long they were, all together in a line like that.*

He said this while Henry was laying down his chain to measure the swamp, so perhaps one thing had reminded him of the other. Ever after it was hard for Henry not to think of the links in his survey chain as the scales on the back of a serpent.

THE red-winged blackbirds had returned to the reeds, their calls reverberating through their bodies and bending the rushes, so that the choir of them moved the marsh grass this way and that with the strength of their song alone. And after the blackbird had lifted from the reed, it was still bent from the weight of the bird, showed the place where the blackbird had perched and sang. In its attitude it was a memorial to the spirit of the bird that had once alighted there.

HENRY watched, through his spyglass, as a man walked up and down along the same patch of ground by the river. This was the spot where the soldiers had had their muster last fall, where they pitched their tents and made their camp. The man seemed to be looking for loose change, for anything of value that might have fallen from the pockets of the soldiers, or been left behind when they broke camp. He was a well-dressed man, with suit and hat—fallen on hard times perhaps, or simply an opportunist who had found an opportunity? It hardly mattered which, thought Henry, the glass held steady to his eye as he watched the stranger methodically treading the ground, his head bent and his hands held stiffly at his sides. If this man had dreamed of finding riches in this spot, would it happen? Did thinking something shape it into reality? Did this treasure hunter have more of a chance of finding treasure than someone walking in this same spot who was not looking for it?

WHEN the train first came to Concord, it terrified the animals. The cows and horses would race from one side of their pasture to the other, the birds would take to the skies, even the fish would skitter upstream when the locomotive shook the ground in its passing.

But now when Henry was looking into the stream, able to see more than usual because of the low-water spring, he noticed that the fish did not move when the train thundered by. They held still in their small school, even as the water above them rippled slightly with the heavy approach of the steel locomotive.

THERE was something about this spring that was distinct from the others, but Henry couldn't decide exactly what it was that made the difference.

I seem to have more time to explore, he said to Sophia.

You are moving slower.

Am I?

Your tread is heavier on the stairs at night, she said. *You seem more tired in the mornings.*

But I don't feel tired.

Indeed, Henry felt strangely energized, but it was an energy that gave him added access to stillness, not one that sent him scampering through the woods and fields. It was an energy that calmed rather than animated.

One evening he sat down by a small bed of bluets, just three feet by two feet, and counted the flowers. They were jammed right up against one another, so tightly packed that he could not see the ground beneath them. He counted and watched a humblebee rolling from flower head to flower head, gathering pollen. The bee was as methodical as Henry, and they finished their tasks at roughly the same time. There were three thousand bluets in that flower bed, the humblebee and Henry having visited each and every one.

THE crows woke him; their ragged calling roused him from his bed and pulled him to the window. They flew over the house and garden, circling the treetops but never settling. A great drift of crows. There must have been close to a hundred, although their constant motion made it impossible to count them. The birds seemed so restless, and their insistent cries almost sounded angry, or at least irritated.

I wish I spoke crow, said Henry at breakfast.

When crows fly over the house, my father used to say, it is an ill omen for those who live there, said Cynthia.

I meant speaking with crows, not speaking about them, said Henry.

Cynthia looked confused.

Mother, said Sophia, scraping butter across her toast, *Henry means that this morning he wants to be a crow.*

HENRY took his boat out after dinner, rowing upriver and then drifting back down, his oars shipped. There was a fog along the banks, lying so thick and low that it seemed a kind of shadow at the edge of the river. He could hear water dripping from the nearby trees, the purr of frogs upstream, and the tap of fish hitting the underside of the lily pads. He wondered if it was colder where the fog hung, and what the fish were eating on the lily pads, but where once he would have rowed into the band of mist, or put his hand into the water to feel along the underside of the pad, now he just sat still. Wondering didn't always need an answer.

MORE and more he was interested in the small particulars—the blue flower, the drift of rain, the single note of a black-bird—and less inclined towards the larger world, where talk of full-scale war was bubbling up with each new clash between pro-slavery forces and the abolitionists.

I don't seem to have as much energy for outrage, he said to Sophia. *But I always have enough energy for praise.*

A Mrs. Miles had taken in two woodchucks and Henry went over to see them. There had been four babies altogether, but the nest was dug out by a dog, and the mother woodchuck kept pushing the babies out towards the dog to save herself. Two of the four kits were eaten, and Mrs. Miles, unable to bear further slaughter, chased the dog away and rescued the remaining babies. She took them into her kitchen and put straw down for them by the stove. She fed them bread and milk, which they ate by taking the bread in their forepaws and sitting up on their haunches, the way a squirrel would eat.

They sleep on their heads, said Mrs. Miles. *I leave the kitchen door open for them, but they don't seem to want to go outside.*

Who can blame them? thought Henry. The world outdoors contained their dead siblings, the danger of dogs, and a mother who thought nothing of sacrificing her young to save herself. Throwing their lot in with Mrs. Miles, eating bread and milk by the warmth of the kitchen stove, seemed an altogether better prospect for the young woodchucks.

In June it rained more than usual. Henry measured the fluctuating height of the rivers and ponds. He watched a thunderstorm with a downpour so heavy that he could not see through the rain. It bounced off the roofs and flattened the gardens in an instant, as though water was being shovelled out of the sky.

After he measured the height of the rivers and ponds, Henry moved on to taking temperatures there. Walden was seventy-one degrees on the bottom near the shore, and seventy-seven degrees on the surface a rod away from the bank. He even took the temperature of the family well after pumping and found it to be a cool forty-nine degrees.

Henry measured the growth of a white pine shoot over the heat of the summer. On June 19 it was sixteen and a quarter inches high, moving up to twenty and three-quarter inches on the twenty-seventh, and then ascending another three inches the following week.

He then set about taking the temperature of all the springs and brooks in the area. He then moved on to the wells of his various neighbours, and drew a correspondence between the forty-nine-degree temperature of all the wells—which was, in fact, the temperature of the water a certain depth inside the earth—and the mean average temperature of Concord.

Henry had always enjoyed the mathematics of the world around him, but now it took precedence over everything else. He could not seem to get enough information about the springs and brooks and ponds and air temperatures. Each time he found out how hot or cold something was, how the temperature fluctuated between one body of water and another, he felt a snag of satisfaction catch in his body. He couldn't stop himself from finding out everything there was to know. It bubbled over in him, like the tumble of the Boiling Spring released from its underground burrow.

He only occasionally stopped to wonder if his desire for exactitude came at the expense of other, unnamed and unexpressed, feelings.

At the height of summer, deep into July, the greens were the darkest of the whole year. Indeed, the mass of trees on shore, when viewed from the water of Walden's Pond, were so dark that they appeared as shadows.

Henry and Edward went to Wayland to visit a taxidermist who had a great collection of birds, even some from the far north. The birds were beautiful and impressive, but the taxidermist seemed less interested in who the birds were than in how he killed them before stuffing them.

He gestured to a little auk.

Shot that one on a pond on the Assabet, he said, *and managed to kill another one there with a paddle.*

He pointed to a petrel.

I shot that in Philadelphia, and the bittern over there was killed on the river meadows near my house.

Henry tired of the taxidermist's boasting after half an hour. He left Edward in the parlour listening to the catalogue of slaughter, and wandered outside into the garden, in search of a living bird.

In August Henry and Ellery decided to climb Monadnock. They took as few supplies as possible. Henry fit all of what he needed into a knapsack and in the pockets of his coat. They took the train to Troy and set out on foot from there, walking on roads and paths until those turned into fields. Then the fields ran into bogs, and once through the bogs, the ground rose and became studded with granite and groves of black spruce trees growing out of the powdered stone of the old mountain.

The first night they made a lean-to of spruce branches and built a fire at the entranceway to help dry their wet boots and socks, soaked through from the bog walking. They ate salt beef and bread, some blueberries that Henry had found growing on the slopes. The fire was cheerful and the green walls of their makeshift cave seemed as reassuring as the sculpted walls of the finest mansion.

What more is there to need? asked Henry, stretching his bare feet out towards the flames.

This is why I like going on a journey with you, said Ellery. *You are satisfied with the smallest of pleasures, the briefest of comforts.*

Henry lay awake under his blanket long enough to hear the cry of a nighthawk, and woke in the morning to the sound of human voices floating around their shelter, although no people were visible.

They climbed through fog and ended up on a plateau where there were tracts upon tracts of blueberries.

Ah, said Henry, *now the morning voices make sense.*

The second night they made camp on a rock ledge. The trees were sparser now, but there were still clumps of them, and all the stone outcroppings looked so similar that when

Ellery went out in the night to relieve his bladder, he had trouble finding his way back.

All the rocks look the same in the dark, he said, stumbling into the crevice where they were bedding down for the night.

In the morning there were more voices, and a steady stream of people walking to the blueberry meadows or to the summit and then back down again. It seemed that climbing Monadnock was more of a family outing than an adventurous botanical expedition.

Henry tried to ignore the boisterous laughter and concentrated on documenting the plant life he found on the slopes. He was very excited to discover cranberries growing among the blueberries, and they ate handfuls of these throughout the day, although Ellery pronounced them too sour in comparison to the blueberry and refused them at breakfast the following morning.

The summit was spectacular, in spite of the other people scattered along the rocky ridge. They could see right through to Vermont and the Green Mountains and beyond. Two ponds miles distant were so blue and still that Henry and Ellery could see the reflection of the nearby trees in them from the top of the mountain.

We're closer to the sun up here, said Henry. He could feel the power of being this high above the earth he normally trod upon. They were in the realm of the gods. He briefly thought of John, of how much his brother would have enjoyed the camping and the climb, this godlike view from the top of the world.

Some of the families were picnicking on the summit. Men had brought chisels with them and were busy carving their names into the rocky surface. Children ran shrieking to the edge, taunting one another to go farther, until their mothers' voices calmly called them back.

Henry and Ellery were planning to camp in their spot from the previous night, which was not far from the summit, so they could linger on the ridge while the families had to fold their blankets and begin the long trek down, leaving enough afternoon light to carry them safely to the bottom of the mountain.

It was a botanizer's paradise on Monadnock. Henry found lambkill and goldthread, a grass called blue-joint, and a variety of ferns and lichens. He wrote everything down in his notebook, sometimes using the microscope he had brought with him to accurately identify a sedge or flower.

The trip was glorious, although Henry couldn't resist scrutinizing his packing and provision list after they were home again in Concord. His one pair of socks had been invaluable, but he never had occasion to wear his flannel shirt. The sleeping blanket, although necessary, would have been of better use if it had been stitched into a bag. The salt beef and tongue they had brought to eat could have been minimized to just the beef, and the eighteen hard-boiled eggs were a complete mistake, as they didn't keep. They had had too much sugar and tea, but just enough bread, and they could have made good use of more dense, sweet cake.

HENRY walked over to Emerson's after supper his first day back, to tell him about the excursion.

It's a well-climbed mountain, is it not? said Emerson, which was a remark that pre-Monadnock Henry would have found off-putting, but now he found he could just ignore it.

They climb for the view, he said. *I climbed for the mountain. And look at what I found there.* He opened his notebook to show Emerson his botanical list.

There was a scratching sound behind them. It was too loud for mice and it seemed to be right in the room with them.

Behind the picture, I think, said Henry. They walked over to the painting on the wall of Emerson on his camping trip in 1858 and slowly lifted it from its hanger. There, on the panelling behind it, was a large bat. The tips of its hairs were covered in white, so that it looked as if it was coated with spiderwebs.

Hoary bat, said Henry. *You open the window and I'll cover it with my shirt to get it out.*

Emerson did as he was bidden, and the bat was quickly and efficiently restored to the outside world. In that moment, the moment of the bat, they were the friends they once had been long ago, and Henry realized that the friendship was still there. It was just hidden from view, but at the right angle, in the right light, it swam back into focus.

HENRY went to measure the skin of a Canada lynx that had been killed just north of Concord. It was an unusual animal to see locally, and he was interested to see the hide. For weeks there had been reports of a strange beast in the area. A little girl who was picking huckleberries told of an animal that jumped over her and bounced away. No one believed her story, but then a man told of hearing the eerie cry of an unknown animal at night, and another talked of seeing a large cat on the edge of a pond.

The farmer who killed the lynx made much of his heroics in shooting it. He had to reload and fire three times, finally dispatching the cat with the butt of his gun. But it was clear to Henry that the man had always had the upper hand, so he tried not to engage in conversation and set about measuring the size of the lynx. The farmer had stuffed the skin with hay and boiled the skull to clean it before shoving it back into position within the hide.

It was not quite as big an animal as one would suppose from the farmer's talk of heroically shooting it to death. In fact, from nose to tail it was only about three and a half feet long and stood just nineteen inches at the shoulder. But an animal in motion was a different thing altogether from one that had been stilled in death. Henry could see how anyone would be afraid at encountering the lynx, but it annoyed him that it was never presented this way—as fear—but was instead turned into a tale of bravery.

Later, Henry went back to take a leg from the carcass and boil it down for the bone. The meat of the animal smelled good, like the best mutton, as the leg knocked around in the pot of bubbling water, but the meat was too old to safely eat, even if Henry had wanted to.

All that week and the next, there was talk of the lynx, and talk of other large cats that had been spotted or killed nearby throughout the years. The idea of wild animals thrilled people, but the reality of them made every man rush for his gun.

A local citizen had started a small museum, and Henry walked over to have a look at the latest additions, given by the last surviving member of the Hosmer family, a distant relative of his friend Edmund. The woman had contributed several artifacts to the little museum, but the one that intrigued Henry the most was a linen bag filled with stones. Each of the stones was the exact weight of a pound, a half-pound, a quarter-pound, and so on, and were used as weights by the family as needed. The stones had been collected locally, perhaps even from the shores of Walden Pond, and they were evidence to Henry of the old ways of living, which were closer to the earth and therefore, in his opinion, more virtuous.

THE butternuts began to fall from the trees, taking down September with them. The sound of them hitting the ground was percussive, the round weight of them making an almost melodious thud onto the earth beneath.

The butternuts fell and the first frost blackened the garden. Leaves hit other leaves on their way down from the trees, the whole cascade sounding like rain. Everything fell, but the milkweed rose on the winds, floating right past Henry's bedroom window as he leaned out over the sill to watch the flimsy silken strands wend their way heavenward.

THE colours this autumn seemed particularly vivid. The maples burned with an otherworldly fire, each one distinct in its pattern of flame. Each one as bright as a struck match.

Henry rowed up the river one day and noticed a young woman rowing a boat behind him. Later, when he saw her on a street in town, and spied the bright red maple leaf she held in her hand, he knew exactly from which tree she had plucked it.

HENRY became momentarily obsessed with oaks and acorns, even going so far as to eat the different acorns from the various kinds of oaks. Most were bitter, even when boiled, but the acorn from the white oak was tolerable and at least as good as a chestnut.

Even though they had not discussed it between them, it turned out that Sophia was also going through an oak and acorn phase. She had been amassing a collection of acorns, mostly taken from the cemetery, Sleepy Hollow. She invited Henry into her room to look at them.

Impressive, said Henry, for the acorns filled every flat surface in the room, grouped into clusters on top of Sophia's dresser and writing table.

I had wanted to sketch them, said Sophia, *but they do not last very long. Look, some of these are turning mouldy already.* She pointed to a small knot of acorns from a white oak, their shells darkening with decay.

The squirrels will be disappointed if they have stored these to sup on in the middle of winter, she said.

Henry picked up one of the acorns, pushing against the soft spot with his thumb.

But by burying them, those squirrels are planting our future forests, he said. *A much more worthwhile pastime.*

DANIEL wrote to Henry about the colour of the autumn leaves, then again about the attitude of plants after a frost, then again to report the first instance of ice covering a puddle. When he wrote a fourth time, he chastised Henry for not writing back soon enough and for ignoring his request that Henry come to visit him. He also hoped that he had not offended Henry, although perhaps he had, because the last time they were together he felt that his nerves were aggravated, which was made worse by his smoking, which, he wanted to make sure Henry knew, he had now given up.

I never promised to correspond with you, Henry wrote back. *We have some things in common, it is true, but in others, we are nothing more than strangers.*

He did not like this feeling of inequality, that Daniel wanted more from him than he was willing to give. It was an awful feeling to introduce into any friendship, and Henry often felt it acutely in his friendship with Daniel. He knew he had been rude in his rebuff, but he wanted to stop Daniel from pushing him to respond, instead of allowing him to respond at his leisure.

THERE was work to be had surveying woodlots, as land had become more valuable and landowners were parcelling up what they had and offering some of it up for sale. Many of these woodlots had the stumps from older trees on them, and Henry often counted the rings to determine the age at which the tree had been felled. Many of the stumps were young trees, twenty-six years old at most, but there were some larger white pine stumps, one of which had an impressive ninety rings. Henry counted 116 rings on a white oak and 135 on a pitch pine. There were several chestnut stumps whose rings indicated they were well over a hundred years old. When all the large timber was being felled, these would have been young trees and left standing.

The counting of the tree rings was calming to Henry. He stood before a stump and dragged his finger slowly across it as he said the numbers out loud like an incantation. The meditative murmuring blocked out other thoughts and kept the moment firmly here, in the cold morning of the woodlot, head bowed over the tree stump, muttering a numeric prayer.

WHEN Henry told a man in town about the Canada lynx he had recently visited, the man said to him, *Pity. If you had been the one to kill it, you could have got the reward.*

What reward?

Ten dollars from the state.

A magnificent wild creature whittled down by commerce to a number, as was everything else wild and free in this world Henry lived in, and sometimes utterly despised.

AFTER measuring stumps, Henry moved on to cataloguing the different varieties of blueberries. This he did from memory, as it was December and the blueberry was no longer growing in the wild.

He was also working on a talk about the colour of the fall leaves, called "Autumnal Tints," which he was to give at the Lyceum in the middle of the month. Bronson Alcott came to call when he was still suffering from a bad cold, and gave it to Henry, so that when it was time to deliver the lecture, Henry was ill and had to drag himself through the talk.

The cold turned to influenza and Henry remained indoors, did not go on his usual walkabout to see where the ice had appeared, or how deep the snow was in the woods. But Ellery came to visit him on his sickbed and informed him that Walden was first frozen over on December 16.

Christmas came and went. Cynthia was also ill and abed, so celebrating was a muted affair. The new year arrived and Henry still hadn't recovered. He lay in bed and looked out his attic window. He could see the tops of the pine trees in the garden, their tops weighted down with snow and bent almost double. It seemed that the slightest addition to their burden of snow would snap them, but instead there was a warm day and the treetop snow melted. The pines sprang back to their original position with no stoop or bend to show the snow's effect.

BORED of being indoors, Henry asked for visitors, and his friend Horace came to see him, bringing him the contents of a crow's stomach. The crow had been killed two days previous, and Horace had kept the stomach in alcohol to preserve it. Henry sat up in bed and picked through the contents with a pair of tweezers. There were pieces of apple, skunk cabbage berries, bits of acorns, a few small bones (perhaps from a mouse or frog?), and a tiny pebble, which was perhaps mistaken by the crow for a berry.

Later, Horace brought Henry a screech owl that he had caught in his barn. Another friend brought a stick that had a hole through it made by a woodpecker.

Ellery dropped by to report on the depth of the snow. He sat beside Henry's bed while Henry coughed and coughed.

It has been ten weeks, said Ellery, *since you were out in the world.*

Henry's coughing sputtered to a stop. He took a breath to steady himself.

Are you growing tired of being my ears and eyes? he asked.

Not in the least. But I welcome the day when you are on your feet again.

It is a long bout of influenza, said Henry, to which Ellery did not reply.

1861~1862

I n February Henry was able to rise and go about his business in the house, although he was still not strong enough to venture outdoors. He wrote in his journal and worked on an essay about trees. He played with the new kitten that had recently joined the Thoreau household, and enjoyed watching her double-jointed antics.

By month's end, after ten weeks abed, he was outside again, sauntering in the warm sun and hearing the first bluebird of the season as he walked down the Boston road. When he got back home, there was a letter from Daniel, who seemed to have forgotten their tiff and had also heard a bluebird. He wrote a couplet to Henry about it:

The bluebird has come, now let us rejoice!
This morning I heard his melodious voice.

Winter seemed to have vanished. The air was warm and the sun was strong. Concord was churning with bluebirds, a great wheel of birds above Henry's head when he walked out into the glorious world.

HENRY was still not strong enough to make the trek to Walden Pond, but Ellery dutifully reported to him that, although only mid-March, there was no more ice on the surface, and the pond was all open water except for Deep Cove. This was earlier than Henry could ever remember the ice breaking up. Other ponds remained frozen.

Why this year? he said to Ellery.

Ellery shrugged.

More snow cover? he suggested.

The snow had come early, before the ground was properly frozen, so perhaps there had been no real ice on Walden to begin with, just a piling on of snow. But it was hard for Henry to let go of the feeling that his not being able to visit Walden Pond, for the first winter since he was a very young child, had something to do with the early melt.

AUNT Sophia, now entering her eightieth year, told a story one night in the parlour about her long-ago dog.

He was just a scrap, she said. *All black and with only half a tail. His name was Bob. We lived in Keene then, and once when I had to leave on a steamer for Boston, he followed me all the way to the docks. I could not persuade him to turn back. It was a good fifty miles.*

What happened when you boarded the ship? asked Henry. *Did he follow you there?*

He wasn't allowed, said Aunt Sophia, *but he didn't even try. He just turned and headed back for home.*

The dog didn't follow you, said Sophia. *He escorted you. He might have felt it was his duty to see you safely on board the steamer.*

Yes, said Aunt Sophia. *He might have felt that. He was a remarkable dog, and I remember him as clearly tonight as though he were in the room with us now.*

There were many stories told these nights in the Thoreau household. Because of Henry's illness, he had been more with his family than usual. Perhaps they had been telling more stories to cheer him up? Whatever the reason, he enjoyed the winter nights of fires and tales.

Your grandmother's second husband, Captain Minott, began Cynthia one night, *used to roast and eat a line of wild apples every evening before bed. And he took to bed with him a quart of new milk that he set down at the head of the bed. He would wake in the night and drink from it, and by morning it was gone. Your grandmother only knew he had died because she woke one night and turned in bed and saw that the milk jug was still full.*

HORACE, who was not really a close friend to Henry, had nevertheless taken his task of entertaining him during his illness very seriously. He brought over the contents of a bullfrog's stomach, which contained a striped snake measuring twenty inches. Next, he brought a fish with a mouse and beetles in its belly, then a black duck's crop containing grass and weeds.

In April Horace came to the door with a dead hermit thrush, then a bufflehead duck. Next, he delivered a pigeon hawk, two small pewees, a white-throated sparrow, a Wilson's thrush, and a myrtle bird.

You have to stop him, said Cynthia. *Our front parlour is beginning to look like a taxidermist's showroom.*

BOTH Henry and his doctor came to the conclusion that a journey was what was needed to shake the cough. Henry meant to go to Minnesota, by way of New York State and Niagara Falls. His family insisted on his having a travelling companion, and Horace was more than happy to oblige. They set out in early May. After months of being housebound, Henry felt the thrill of travel more keenly than usual. Every conversation he had en route was fascinating. Every scene he saw from the carriage was spellbinding and worth noting.

The hotel they stayed in at Niagara was less than half a mile from the falls, but Henry mistook the sound of the falls for a steam train or the nearby factories.

It is because I have never heard Niagara Falls before, he said to Horace. *The roar of the water does not sound natural to me, but rather sounds like clamour from the human world.*

From Niagara Falls they travelled to Detroit. Henry thought Lake Ontario looked more like a sea than a lake. He saw great stretches of marsh full of blackbirds and bulrushes, and a red-bellied woodpecker in undulating flight.

From Detroit they moved on to Chicago, with its limestone buildings and the milky waters of Lake Michigan.

The travel did not shake loose Henry's illness. His chest was still wracked by cough, and he had lost both weight and strength, but mentally he was cheered by the new sights and sounds on the journey. He marvelled in the rolling prairie near Winnebago, and the flowering crabapple trees through much of Illinois.

They took a river boat from Dunleith into Minnesota, arriving in St. Paul on May 26. Here they remained for several days. Henry looked at trees and visited a doctor, listened to the song of a horned lark soaring above the prairie. Horace shot two rose-breasted grosbeaks, two chipmunks, and a gopher.

In June Horace and Henry settled into a cottage on the edge of Lake Calhoun. It was warm and pleasant and the days were easy ones, but Henry wasn't recovering. He was not exactly getting worse, but he wasn't getting any better either. An excursion to find some wild crabapple trees was more tiring than energizing, though he continued to think about the pink froth of their blossom for days afterwards.

Horace tried valiantly to keep on top of the ravenous need his mother had to correspond with him.

I only answered her latest letter yesterday, he complained to Henry, *and here's another one in the post!*

Just repeat what you said yesterday, said Henry. *She might not even notice.*

AT the end of June they were homeward bound, reversing their steps to make the multi-stage journey back to Concord. They travelled through Toronto in Canada, a city rising out of the stumps that surrounded it. Henry botanized there for part of a day and discovered speedwell growing near Toronto College, the tiny blue flowers like the smallest of stars set among the deep green leaves of the plant.

As the train slowed on its approach to the station in Concord, Henry saw a group of men with a large net walking towards a dead tree on which there was a flock of passenger pigeons.

You can get a hundred at a time using that method, said Horace approvingly. *They aren't expecting the net.*

The birds looked stately, with their long tails and rose-coloured breasts. They sat calmly on the branches of the dead tree, patiently awaiting their fate.

When Henry arrived back home, he discovered a long letter from Daniel, who had recently, and fervently, converted to Christianity and now believed, he wrote, in the existence of an *Evil Spirit*, which had come to do battle for Daniel's soul.

Henry was glad to hear from Daniel, but it took him until the middle of August to write back. When he did, aside from expressing surprise at Daniel's recent conversion, he asked if Daniel's multiple invitations to visit were still valid, and said that he would like to make the journey to see him the following week.

THE first evening at the Ricketson house, Henry entertained the family with talk of his two-month sojourn to Minnesota and his visit to Niagara Falls. The next morning he walked with Daniel the short distance from the house to his shanty, and they continued their conversation there.

The shanty had not changed since Henry was first in it. He thought of how long ago now it was that he had lived in his own little house at Walden Pond, and he wondered why he had given it up. Being in Daniel's shanty made Henry miss and remember his life at Walden.

Your hut is reassuringly the same, he said.

Daniel looked confused. *Why would I change it?*

Indeed. Why would you?

They settled into chairs and resumed their conversation from the night before. Occasionally Daniel veered the talk towards Christianity and his new-found faith, but Henry adroitly steered it away from that shoal, where he did not wish to flounder.

Mostly it was pleasant to visit with Daniel. They took walks in the woods, to a nearby pond, to an old farmhouse. The walks were not as long as they once might have been, but Henry managed them well enough. The coughing tired him and he had to rest more during the day, but he was still able to do most of what he wanted. He was still able to feel like himself.

On the second day, Daniel took Henry into town to sit for an ambrotype.

Your family will be glad to have so recent a likeness of you, he said, not voicing what they both knew, that it would probably be the last photograph Henry would ever pose for.

Henry sat in the chair as directed by the photographer and stared into the eye of the camera. What was it that he was looking at? Whose eye was the eye of the camera? Who saw him?

WHEN Henry returned from New Bedford, he and Sophia spent a day together at Walden Pond. It was very much like any day they had ever spent together, in that they were involved in their separate activities, occasionally coming together to remark on what Henry was looking at or what Sophia was sketching.

It was a perfect September day, with a pure blue sky and warmth in the air. Henry collected grapes from one of the wild vines near the edge of the pond. Behind him, Sophia drew the trees.

Later they stood at the shore, looking out at the ripples on the pond and listening to the chatter of the birds.

This is my earliest memory, said Sophia. *I was very small and I was here with you and mother and father, practically right here on this very spot. It was a day like this one, and I was holding on to your hand.*

Yes, I remember that day, said Henry. *I have always remembered that day.*

And now I will remember this one also, said Sophia. *For the both of us.*

DANIEL wrote to say that he was sending a doctor to Henry who was experienced in matters of the chest. Then he wrote to say that he had decided to come with the doctor.

The doctor examined Henry and suggested that he take a sea voyage, as the sea air could help him.

No, said Henry. *A sea voyage is not what I plan on doing.*

Then I'm afraid there is not much more I can suggest or do for you.

After the doctor left, Henry and Daniel went bathing at Walden Pond, and spent the next few days visiting Bronson Alcott and Emerson, and walking with Sophia. Daniel went out for a short after-dinner stroll one night in the dark and got lost, returning to the Thoreau house hours later.

Daniel returned home after several days. Edward, who had business out of town, lent Henry one of his horses and a cart, so it would be easier for Henry to travel around. Edward's dog, who was a good friend of the horse, accompanied them on all expeditions. The company of the horse and dog was just as good, Henry thought, as the recent company of Daniel.

On a rainy October day, Henry watched the robins and sparrows feeding from berries and the seeds that had shaken free from the weeds and flowers by the autumn wind. There were so many birds in the garden that their chatter was as loud as animated conversation at a dinner party.

The birds gorged on the seeds and berries, then retreated to the branches of a nearby tree to digest, then chattered and returned to gorge some more. The wheel and whirl of their activity was all so absolutely centred on their bird world that they could care less about the lone human who watched them so intently from his open attic window.

HENRY was too weak for surveying, but in November he inspected a stone bridge in town, to report on its condition to the council. The bridge arched over the Concord where it was but a small stream. Henry nudged his boat under the bridge to inspect the stones and mortar. It was quiet and dark under there. He saw a swallow's neat nest attached to the underside of the arch. When he touched the stones nearby it, they were cold and damp. It was like being inside the mouth of the river, the stacked stones like teeth socketed into the jaw of the old bridge. When Henry coughed, the echo came back to him as the barking of a dog.

FOR much of 1861 the North and the South had been preparing for war over slavery, with the South amassing an army of over a million men. A battle had been fought, but the newly elected President Lincoln had not moved the Northern army into position to fully engage with the South.

This new development brought Henry back into conversation with the larger world. All December he fumed over this lack of engagement, talking politics with Bronson or Emerson, lamenting the failure of Lincoln to act decisively.

How could the war have been going on for months and still not have actually started? he said to Bronson, when he came to call one afternoon.

Later, when Bronson put on his coat and hat in the hallway and prepared to go, Cynthia followed him out onto the doorstep.

How did he seem to you today? she asked.

I think his anger at Lincoln is improving his health, said Alcott. *His complexion is positively glowing.*

THE war did come, finally, with news of it changing every day. Bronson collected his winter apples from his orchard, pressing some into cider and cellaring the rest. He brought Henry an apple and a bottle of cider and the news of the day. Henry drank the cider, but didn't eat the apple right away. He held it in his hands, the round weight so satisfying when he rolled it from palm to palm. He knew he wouldn't live long enough to see how the war turned out, nor probably to taste next year's crop of apples from the Alcott orchard, so the only thing to do was to delay eating this apple for as long as he possibly could.

IT snowed. Henry developed pleurisy, which weakened him further. He sat indoors and watched the snow drift past his window, wind its skein around the trees. Daniel wrote and reported that he had been skating on the ponds around Middleboro and, for the first time in their correspondence, stated that he did not require a reply from Henry. Reading this, Henry was flooded with relief.

Henry worked on his manuscript of "Autumnal Tints," editing it when he had small bursts of energy.

Alek came to visit, but he was drunk, and when Henry opened the front door of the house and saw him on the stoop, red-faced and swaying on his feet, the smell of alcohol perfuming the air between them, he sent him away.

You should just go and slit your throat, he said, and saw Alek's hurt and confused look before he shut the door on him.

He used to be a god to me, Henry said to Sophia. *The chickadees would land on his shoulders. He would feed the wild creatures from his hands.*

Later that week Emerson came to read a poem in progress to Henry. It was ostensibly about a titmouse, but seemed actually to be about a chickadee, and then a phoebe, and perhaps it was a poem about Henry dying. Henry just listened and let the words roll over him, thinking not of Emerson's poem at all, but of Alek sitting on a stump in the woods at Walden Pond, with the light slanting through the trees and the birds flitting about his head.

> *Well, in this broad bed lie and sleep,—*
> *The punctual stars will vigil keep,—*
> *Embalmed by purifying cold;*
> *The winds shall sing their dead-march old,*
> *The snow is no ignoble shroud,*
> *The moon thy mourner, and the cloud.*

Sophia wrote Henry's correspondence for him. He dictated to her his business letters, and she wrote on her own to inform his friends and associates of his declining health.

In a letter to Ticknor and Fields, who would be publishing "Autumnal Tints," and reprinting *Walden,* Henry was adamant that they include an engraving of a scarlet oak and a white oak in the former, both of which he would supply to them.

But you haven't left the house since early December, said Sophia, hesitating over transcribing his declaration. *And it is the middle of winter.*

Do you not think that I will make it until spring?

I'm not sure.

Do you not think I will make it until spring if I am determined to collect the leaves of a scarlet oak and a white oak?

I don't know.

Oh. Henry was quiet for a moment. *Then I suppose,* he said finally, *you had better choose a good example of both from our herbarium, to send along with this letter.*

He was forty-four years old, almost twice the age John was when he died.

DANIEL wrote, sending such a detailed chronicle of the seasonal changes that Henry forgave him every previous grievance. It delighted him to read of the appearance of the first bluebird in Daniel's corner of the world, which had arrived on February 7.

Geese were recorded flying overhead, their progress watched through a spyglass and their direction plotted with a compass. The wind direction was measured and the temperature at the side of Daniel's house was recorded as being forty-six degrees at 3:00 p.m. on March 23. All bird species were catalogued, as was the exact colour of the patches of grass that were now visible in the wake of the retreating snow. Catkins were described in all their plumpness on the willows.

Daniel's happiness at the beginning of spring optimistically coloured the letter, and he prophesized that Henry must be improving and would soon be out of doors himself to experience the pleasing changes.

You should write to him, Henry said to Sophia, *and let him know the truth. He will just invite me to visit otherwise.*

DANIEL wrote again, this time to talk about taking his wife on an excursion to a pine wood, for the piney air contained in such a wood. He wondered if Henry would not benefit from visiting, in reality or by imagination, such a wood. Then he suggested that Henry make a map showing all his familiar routes around Concord. In the next paragraph he described his dreams of the two previous nights. In the first dream he was climbing a mountain with an unnamed companion, who might have been Henry. At the summit they saw two huge birds, who turned into griffins, as big as horses.

In the second dream, Daniel was walking through a filthy village with twisted streets. He opened a door and a terrible smell wafted out to meet his nostrils.

The last part of the letter talked about two men passing by Daniel's window in a buggy, singing the verses of "John Brown," a ballad of the famous abolitionist that had been written the previous year and had become a battle song for the North in the Civil War.

John Brown's body lies a mouldering in the grave,
John Brown's body lies a mouldering in the grave,

John Brown's body lies a mouldering in the grave,
His soul's marching on!

Finally, at the close of the letter, Daniel talked about seeing a cricket on the path to his shanty and flies inside the shanty. Also, geese flying overhead at precisely 4:00 p.m.

The next time Daniel wrote to him, Henry put the letter aside, to open later, if he was still alive. Daniel's energy, even contained inside a letter, was just too much for Henry now.

THE bluebirds and robins sang outside Henry's window. He liked to listen to them with his eyes closed, lying in bed, too weak to rise now.

A young girl came and brought him the first lilac blooms. Sophia ushered the girl upstairs to Henry's bedside, and he took the blooms from her himself.

Let's close our eyes and smell their scent, he said to the child.

They took a spray each and shut their eyes for a moment, inhaling the rich, sweet perfume of the lilac.

There, said Henry, when they opened their eyes again. *Now we will remember that scent forever.*

EMERSON came to read Henry the appreciation of him that Bronson Alcott had written for *The Atlantic Monthly.*

He calls you "a holy man within a Hermitage."

Does he?

The tribute that Alcott had written was so tender and laudatory that Henry, who thought he might mind this obituary written before he had died, could only smile at the words Emerson read to him, and the sentiment they contained.

Ralph.

It felt strange to say his given name after all the years of only referring to him by his surname.

Yes.

Emerson bent his head towards Henry, to receive the blessings of the dying man, or his confession, or his promise of eternal friendship continuing resolutely beyond the grave.

Ralph, said Henry, *I'm going to tell you one of my greatest secrets.*

Yes.

Emerson bent his head even farther, so that his ear was right up against Henry's mouth.

I'm going to tell you where to find the blue snowbird.

On May 5 Henry asked for his friend Edmund Hosmer to come and spend the night with him. Henry feared it might be his last night on earth and wanted to spend it in the company of his oldest friend, the man who had helped him build his cabin at Walden Pond.

Henry, said Edmund, when he entered Henry's bedchamber, *the robins were singing so sweetly all the way here. Louder and more sweetly than usual, I think. Perhaps sweeter than any other year.*

Henry smiled.

Wouldn't it be nice if that were so, he said.

It took effort for him to speak now, so there were large parts of the night when they didn't speak at all. Edmund sat beside Henry's bed while his friend drifted in and out of sleep. When Henry was conscious they listened to the night sounds outside the window together—the shriek of a fox, the hoot of an owl.

Towards morning, when the sky was lightening, Henry opened his eyes.

Edmund, because you are my oldest friend, he said, *I want to give you my most treasured possession.* With effort he reached under his pillow and handed Edmund a book.

It's my memorial copy of A Week on the Concord and Merrimack Rivers, Henry said. *The copy I would have given to John.*

It was only when Edmund had left the Thoreau house and was walking home that he opened the book and saw, taped to the inside front cover, a lock of John Thoreau's hair.

←

HENRY asked Sophia to read to him from his book about his river trip with John. He lay in bed, eyes closed, with the warmth of the spring sun creeping through the trees into his room, birdsong bubbling away in the background.

It all unspooled away from him. And then swam back, gloriously transformed.

The bubble of birdsong was the music of his father's flute, each note striking the air at just the right angle.

The wind at the top of Fairhaven Cliffs pushing against his chest was the pressure of his mother's hands holding him close to her.

The Boiling Spring rattled with the songs Helen sang with her anti-slavery choir.

The straight young trees were Alek.

The red oak leaf, with its points and bays, was the topography of the ocean shore. If there were but lighthouses on all those points, and the bays were silted and shallow, then Margaret Fuller would never have drowned.

The colour of the fiery hangbird's breast was the light through the shanty walls that summer when Henry lived with Charles on the edge of Flint's Pond and they lay in their beds and talked well into the night, and there was no other happiness.

Apple blossom frothing on the trees was the laughter of Lidian and the children in the summer garden.

Emerson was the bright North Star.

The beat of a swan's wing was the pace of Ellery's stride as he walked ahead of Henry up the mountain and then back down again.

The scratch of crickets was the sound of Sophia sketching, the noises she made moving her pencil across the paper.

The blue of winter light was the colour of John's eyes.

John waved his hand from across the yard—a pine bending in the breeze.

John waved his hand, and Henry rose to go and meet him.